Janice Lynn has a Masters in
Nursing from Vanderbilt University,
and works as a nurse practitioner
in a family practice. She lives in
the southern United States with her
husband, their four children, their
Jack Russell—appropriately named
Trouble—and a lot of unnamed dust
bunnies that have moved in since
she started her writing career. To
find out more about Janice and her
writing visit janicelynn.com.

Also by Janice Lynn

After the Christmas Party…
Flirting with the Doc of Her Dreams
New York Doc to Blushing Bride
Winter Wedding in Vegas
Sizzling Nights with Dr Off-Limits
It Started at Christmas…
The Nurse's Baby Secret
The Doctor's Secret Son
A Firefighter in Her Stocking
A Surgeon to Heal Her Heart

Discover more at millsandboon.co.uk.

HEART SURGEON TO SINGLE DAD

JANICE LYNN

MILLS & BOON

First published in Great Britain 2018
by Mills & Boon, an imprint of HarperCollins*Publishers*
1 London Bridge Street, London, SE1 9GF

Large Print edition 2019

© 2018 Janice Lynn

ISBN: 978-0-263-07814-5

MIX
Paper from
responsible sources
FSC
www.fsc.org   FSC® C007454

This book is produced from independently certified
FSC™ paper to ensure responsible forest management. For
more information visit www.harpercollins.co.uk/green.

Printed and bound in Great Britain
by CPI Group (UK) Ltd, Croydon, CR0 4YY

In loving memory of my papa,
Floyd Green.

CHAPTER ONE

"I'M A DOCTOR, you know." No, the flight attendant didn't know, but Natalie Sterling was determined to make it on time to her presentation.

She'd heard of airlines overbooking flights, but it had never affected her. Until now.

"A pediatric heart surgeon," she added, hoping to gain empathy. Natalie couldn't recall having pulled that card before, but she wasn't one to no-show a speaking commitment if she could help it. "Bumping me to a later flight doesn't work."

The stewardess shook her head. "There's nothing I can do. It was in the agreement when you purchased your ticket that if the plane is overbooked you would have to take a later flight."

Taking a deep breath, Natalie stared at the pretty thirty-something blonde in her crisp uniform. It wasn't the woman's fault.

"It's urgent I go on this flight." She heard the

almost pleading tone, but was beyond caring. She needed to get to Miami this afternoon.

"We're sorry for any inconvenience, but you're going to have to exit the plane." The forced smile on the attendant's face warned that further argument was futile and the woman was losing her patience.

If only Natalie could have kept her flight the evening before, instead of having to delay her departure. Still, she'd been needed for an emergency surgery, and her patients came first. Always.

"What if I refuse to give up my seat?"

The attendant's obligatory smile disappeared. "I would be forced to call Security." Her tone warned Natalie would regret such a decision. "They would escort you off the plane. Are you refusing?"

Visions of herself being dragged off the plane, kicking and screaming that they had the wrong person, had Natalie cringing. Yeah, that splattered all over the news wouldn't impress Memphis Children's Hospital's board.

Feeling much like she was being punished for a crime she hadn't committed, Natalie closed her laptop, unclasped her seatbelt and pulled her case out from under the seat in front of her.

"I'm not refusing, I just wondered if it was an option."

"It's not," she was assured, the stewardess's eyes still narrowed.

"Fine." Not really, but apparently she had no choice. "But you have to get me to Miami this afternoon."

She gathered her things and pulled her carry-on bag back out from the overhead compartment.

Seeing that Natalie wasn't going to give them any further trouble, the flight attendant's obligatory smile returned. "Yes, ma'am. We'll do all we can to get you to your destination as quickly as possible."

As she was passing through the first-class section, a man glanced up from his phone. He turned his head toward her about the time she registered who he was, and Natalie's gaze collided with his.

Her breath caught. Just as it had done when their gazes had met in the airport waiting area.

No matter how she'd tried, she hadn't been able to keep from glancing his way and they'd made eye contact several times. She'd felt an instant attraction, had thought that if her best friends were there they'd have pushed her to cross the room and strike up a conversation because they thought she needed a vacation fling. Natalie being Natalie, she hadn't done anything more than fight to keep her focus on her upcoming presentation rather than on the intriguingly handsome man.

She bet *he* never got bumped from his flight. No one would dare.

There was something dark and dangerous in those ice-blue eyes. Maybe it was his inky black hair and tan skin that contrasted so dramatically with those frosty blues that gave him such a startlingly handsome look, like he belonged in some paranormal movie where he'd shapeshift into a sexy mythical being who preyed on unsuspecting women who were powerless to resist his allure.

Natalie felt his pull, felt his power, and a sexual intensity flashed through her mind. No doubt, he'd have looked into the flight attendant's eyes and told her to go pick someone else and she'd have answered, Yes, sir, and can I get you anything else with that?

Just like Jonathan.

Bleh. She wasn't going to think about her boyfriend.

Ex-boyfriend.

The lying, cheating scumbag.

Literally.

Casting one last look at Mr. Dark and Dangerous, who was watching her with the same expression with which one might watch an accident unfold, probably wondering if she was going to cause a ruckus and delay his flight, she sighed. Not a good start to her little mini-vacation wrapped up in teaching a workshop at a medical conference. As long as she got to Miami in time to give her presentation, everything would be fine.

Despite rushing through Miami Airport and hiring a taxi driver who'd taken her request to get her to her hotel as fast as possible, literally, Natalie missed the time of her presentation.

Frazzled from the delay, then the mad dash, she'd dropped her bags with the bellhop, then quietly snuck into the auditorium and slid into the back row to catch the end of what they'd filled her spot with. Settling into her seat, she glanced to the front of the auditorium and almost fell out of her chair.

No way.

Not even possible.

She was hallucinating.

Maybe she'd fallen during her jaunt through

the airport, bumped her head and was in a coma, about to have a fantastic fantasy.

Must be, because the speaker at the front of the room was him.

Mr Dark and Dangerous from the plane.

He would be a fantastic fantasy.

But why was he teaching her class? And smiling and charming the crowd as if he were a natural-born motivational speaker rather than the dark, sexy overlord she'd painted him out to be on the plane? Seriously, the man was discussing heart deformities and yet you'd think he was revealing the secret of longevity by the way the attendees were on the edge of their seats.

Even as passionate as she was about surgical neonatal heart disease treatment modalities, she didn't think it was the topic that was mesmerizing the crowd.

It was him.

As he spoke, his gaze met with hers and recognition flashed in those unusual ice-blue eyes that somehow didn't fit with his pleasant expression. Probably because she'd pegged him as shadowy and menacing, not smiling and charming.

He was smiling. And charming. And had a voice that should be reading the books she downloaded to her smartphone from time to time to listen to at night. What a way to fall asleep.

Dark and dangerous or smiling and charming, the man oozed sex. She wasn't a woman who got hot and bothered from just looking at a guy. Or even hot and bothered from a whole lot of guy effort, but this man made her think S-E-X.

Hot, sweaty, body-slapping, can't-catch-your-breath sex.

Which was quite disturbing because Jonathan hadn't affected her this potently. Ever. Sex had been good, pleasurable, but just the thought of it hadn't set her nerve-endings on fire.

His presentation didn't pause, but his gaze lingered on hers, flashing with an awareness that made her nerve-endings burn. Hot, out-of-control burn.

He was gorgeous. Perhaps more so than any man she'd ever seen in real life.

Perhaps? Ha. Life had not thrown men like him into her path. Ever. As much as she'd cared for and found him attractive, Jonathan didn't have a thing on this guy. Not even on this guy's worst day and Jonathan's best. Mr. Dark and Dangerous exuded pheromones by the bucketful. His bucket ran over and was flooding the auditorium.

Natalie picked up a mini-sized notepad with the hotel's logo at the top and fanned her face. *Mercy.*

He finished his presentation, then did a question-and-answer session, fielding each question with ease, much more smoothly than she'd have done. She'd have been battling nerves at presenting to a room full of peers.

Whoever he was, he didn't look nervous. Dark, sexy overlords probably didn't get nervous. When the power of the universe was at your handsome fingertips, why sweat?

As she was doing. Her reaction had surprised her at the airport, on the plane, and even more so now that she'd seen the allure of his smile.

Applause filled the room. Natalie clapped, too. He'd done an excellent job, as if he'd been meant to give the presentation all along. She owed him for filling in when she wasn't there.

At the applause, the workshop moderator stood. "Thank you, Dr. Coleman, for volunteering to present when the vacancy opened." The moderator patted him on the back, shook his hand. "You did an excellent job, Matthew."

"No problem."

The man should really smile more because his face transformed into a work of art. Okay, so dark and dangerous had been a work of art, too, but smiling he was heart-stopping.

"I was glad to help, since I understand Dr. Sterling had travel delays," he continued, not glancing her way, but Natalie felt his awareness of her. As if he had some sixth sense that let him know exactly where she was in the room without those amazing eyes having to focus her way. That sense pervaded her entire being and scorched her insides.

Good grief, the way he affected her. Maybe because she was on the cusp of a huge career leap, maybe because she still felt the sting from Jonathan's betrayal.

Or maybe it was how pheromonally magnetic he was.

Another round of clapping and the group broke for a fifteen-minute break between sessions.

A few attendees moved forward to talk with Dr. Coleman. Natalie should thank him and introduce herself to the workshop moderator, who was also the conference chair, so she could apologize again for her delay.

Dr. Matthew Coleman. She'd never met him.

No way would she have forgotten, so why did that name ring a bell?

Suddenly, her jaw dropped. Impossible. *That* Dr. Matthew Coleman had to be in his fifties at the absolute minimum. Surely. No way could this gorgeous doctor be *that* Dr. Matthew Coleman. It just wasn't feasible that he could be the renowned pediatric heart surgeon whose work she so greatly admired.

No way.

Plus, he'd been on a flight out of Memphis. *That* Dr. Matthew Coleman lived in Boston and headed up a research team making great strides with a robotic laser being developed for surgical use, including in utero. There couldn't be two pediatric heart surgeons by the same name doing innovative in-utero surgical repairs, surely?

That was when what he was saying caught her attention. He was making a comment about the robot that Dr. Matthew Coleman was one of the country's leading experts on.

Yeah, she was about to have a fan-girl moment.

Holy smokes. The gorgeous man she'd been fantasizing about on and off ever since the airport was someone she'd idolized for his brain and surgical skills for almost a decade.

What were the odds of the pretty brunette who'd caught Dr. Matthew Coleman's eye at the airport being his top competition for the hospital position he'd just interviewed for?

Not that Dr. Luiz had told him that, but he'd said there was another contender the hospital had been planning to offer the position to, prior to Matthew's interest. Dr. Natalie Sterling was who the man had repeatedly praised for her surgery skills and dedication to pediatric cardiology. She had to be who the department head had meant and, possibly, why they'd not been willing to meet the conditions Matthew had required to relocate.

Those conditions were the deal-maker—or -breaker.

Relocating to Memphis would decrease his stress by leaps and bounds in some ways, but he still wasn't sure he could give up everything he'd worked to achieve just to make the move in any case. Just because his life had been thrust into total chaos three months ago. Basically, he wanted what he had in Boston, but with less work hours and a new zip code that better fit his personal needs. Anything less and he'd stay where he was.

Which was why he'd contacted Dr. Luiz when a colleague had told him about the upcoming opening at Memphis Children's Hospital. He'd already been toying with the idea of relocating to Memphis to be closer to family—for Carrie, the little girl he now had to take care of, to be closer to family. Closer to people who actually knew how to take care of kids. But he couldn't just step away from his research and career. He wouldn't.

Maybe he should try to convince his mother to move to Boston, again. He wasn't sure what he'd have done if she hadn't been able to stay those first few weeks of Matthew's unexpected push into fatherhood. She'd been so good with Carrie. Why couldn't she have stayed longer?

Or maybe he'd resume interviews for a live-in nanny for the precious four-year-old who was now his sole responsibility. Some older woman who'd successfully raised multiple children and could get a child out of bed, have her dressed, fed, looking presentable, and to preschool on time. Something he continued to struggle with on a daily basis. None of the nannies he'd met

so far had clicked, but surely there was someone out there he'd trust with Carrie?

His gaze connected with Natalie's golden one
and he let out a long breath. Prior to Carrie's
new role in his life, he'd have gotten her number at the airport and made plans to meet.

Instead, for the first time ever, despite his
many previous flights, he'd been sweating getting onto an airplane, his mind filled with all
the things that could go wrong—and recently
had.

Plus, he had a four-year-old girl to think about.

Pursuing relationships with pretty brunettes
wasn't on the cards. He could barely juggle
his current schedule, much less adding someone else to the bedlam. He'd always excelled
at everything he'd done. Who'd have thought it
would be an adorable little kid who'd have him
ready to pull his hair out?

He turned back to the portly gentleman from
Shriner's Hospital, smiled as they exchanged
business cards, then heard a voice behind him.

"Why didn't you tell me who you were?"

Knowing who it was even before their eyes
made contact, Matthew turned, his gaze connecting to the brunette's. He could feel her pres-

ence as succinctly as if he had sonar outlining her shapely curves. "Excuse me?"

Her face took on a sheepish expression. "Sorry, I guess there was no reason for you to tell me, but I can't believe the coincidence that you'd be on my plane."

Not a coincidence, but there wasn't a reason to tell her about his meeting with Memphis Children's Hospital and that the job she was vying for had been offered to him. He'd turned it down when his terms couldn't be met. Natalie need never know she wasn't always the top contender.

He smiled, thinking she was even more attractive up close. Her eyes sparkled like sunshine hitting honey. Her skin was smooth and naturally tan with a few light freckles scattered across her nose. Her hair flowed silky and dark to just beneath her shoulders.

She wore a red skirt suit with a crisp white shirt that loosely hugged her curves.

"I see the airline was able to book you another flight." Perhaps it was wrong to tease, but he couldn't resist. Something about her made him want to tease, to watch her facial expressions and burn every detail into his memory.

"Too late to make it on time, though," she

mused, her painted red lips curving into a smile. "Thank you for filling in."

Matthew resisted the urge to loosen his collar. "No problem. I was with the conference coordinator when he was discussing what to do with your time slot. Pediatric heart surgery of any kind is a subject I'm passionate about, so I offered to step in." He grinned. "He jumped at my offer."

"I'm sure." Another flash of those sparkly eyes and dynamic curving of her full lips. "Are you staying for the next presentation?"

At her smile, all his blood traveled south and brain operations came to a halt, making logical thought impossible. Did she have any idea of the power her eyes held to bewitch a man? Absolutely stunning.

"If so, there's an open seat next to mine," she continued. "Maybe you'd like to join me?"

Matthew stared at the biggest temptation he'd ever faced, wished the timing of meeting her had been prior to three months ago, when his life hadn't been in such upheaval. "If not?"

Uncertainty flashed across her face, but then with a determined look, she lifted her chin, stared straight in his eyes, and said, "If not, then maybe we could meet later for the conference opening dinner reception and you could tell me all about your work, because you fascinate me. Your work does, that is."

CHAPTER TWO

NATALIE WAS WAY outside her comfort zone.
But her BFFs would be proud, right? She had
walked up to a man she found enthralling on
paper, sexy in real life, and she'd expressed her
interest in him.

And in his work.

He might think her a fool. For all she knew,
he had a girlfriend.

Duh. Of course a man as gorgeous as Matthew had a girlfriend. What had she been thinking? She'd practically been drooling prior to
finding out who he was, and after? Well, the
man mesmerized.

Not that she'd dreamed in a million years that
she might act on their suggestions, but when
Suzie and Monica told her to have a fling to put
Jonathan out of her mind once and for all, they
should have been more specific. As in, making sure who she wanted wasn't already taken.
Yes, she had noted at the airport that he didn't

have a wedding band, but even that didn't mean anything beyond that he wasn't wearing a ring. The star-struck look in her eyes had probably terrified the poor man.

Still, he didn't look the type to easily scare.

"I have a seat." He turned, gesturing to a spot on the front row.

Ouch. Married, dating, or whatever, she'd been shot down.

Trying not to let her disappointment and embarrassment show, she glanced around and was grateful to see the next speaker at the podium. "Okay, well, it's time to restart, so..."

Awkward.

Not waiting for a response, she high-tailed it to her back row seat to shrivel up and die of humiliation. So much for going after what she wanted.

Ugh. Could this day possibly get worse?

Later that evening, Natalie stared at her reflection in the hotel room mirror.

For a few insane moments, she had let herself be guided by pure feminine interest and she'd made a fool of herself with Matthew Coleman.

Because he was a sexy beast or because of his surgical skills?

Or both?

He was brilliant. She'd read enough of his articles and research to know the man was a genius. That alone would have had her introducing herself, wanting to discuss his work, pick his brain and soak up everything he said.

That he was utterly gorgeous, well, that was a bonus.

Or could have been, had he been interested. She'd thought she'd seen interest, but she must have been wrong.

He wasn't. Had shot down her offer. End of story. Major embarrassment and utter failure at her first show of interest in the opposite sex since her and Jonathan's split, but not the end of the world. The opposite sex wasn't a priority. Her career was and she had that—so no big deal, right?

Still, the conference wasn't so big that she wouldn't bump into Matthew. She'd act as if her invitation had been casual, that she'd only been interested professionally. She was Dr. Natalie Sterling, a pediatric heart surgeon with some pretty fabulous credits to her name, thanks to having met Dr. Luiz during her residency and his having pulled her onto his research team.

No harm done in asking Matthew to dinner. It wasn't as if she'd verbalized that looking at him made her want to take off his clothes and do wild and crazy things.

With one last look in the hotel bathroom mirror, she applied a fresh coat of lipstick, checked to make sure she didn't have any smeared on her teeth, and left the safety of her hotel room to go to dinner. Maybe she'd get lucky and she wouldn't see Matthew this evening.

Or, as her luck for the day would have it, he'd be the first person she saw when she stepped off the elevator.

Seriously, the elevator door slid open and there he was, just outside the elevator bank.

Sometimes life wasn't fair.

The man's looks weren't fair. Those eyes. So unusual. So mesmerizing. So zoned-in on her.

How was she supposed to act professional when he made her giddy as a schoolgirl? Ha. She hadn't been a giddy schoolgirl. She didn't recall ever having felt so inferno-hot inside.

His gaze raked over her red heels, up her bare legs to where her red skirt brushed the tops of her knees. His visual perusal continued, up and beyond to where her waist dipped in beneath her white blouse and matching red jacket. The fire burning in his icy blue eyes had her insides battling the urge to run back to the elevator versus leaping into his arms and ripping off his clothes.

He made her feel alive, hot, very female. That scared her. Probably because she wasn't one for letting her body dictate her actions and he made her body want to act. *Logic*. That was what dictated her life. Logic, and…

Those wicked blue eyes connected with hers. Forget logic.

Her breath caught. Her skin prickled with awareness. Her thighs clenched. Any moment her heart was going to pound its way free of her chest. She might spend most of her time locked away in the sterile confines of the hospital, but she wasn't a fool or oblivious. Desire shone in his eyes and matching want burned within her.

"I was beginning to think you'd changed your mind about dinner." He smiled, his voice deep, warm, drawing her further under his spell. "I'm glad I waited."

Natalie's legs liquefied. She remained upright. Somehow. Matthew had just given her a complete once-over and now he was saying he'd been waiting on her? Had she really awakened from the light nap she'd taken, sitting on her room's balcony?

"I have a table near the front and asked a couple to save our seats," he continued. "I hope that was okay." When she nodded, he placed his hand low on her back and guided her toward the hotel ballroom, where their dinner keynote presentation would take place. "You look lovely, by the way."

His hand burned through the material of her suit, searing her skin with its warmth and making her feel a little woozy. His actions were familiar, as if he had the right to touch her. Obviously he did, because she wasn't complaining.

"I looked for you after Dr. Epsteiner's lecture, but never spotted you, not then or at any other point this afternoon."

Insides rattled at his admission, Natalie focused on each step she took and prayed she didn't stumble in her heels. Carefully, she made her way across the room. Why hadn't she slipped on her trusty flats prior to coming down?

She'd skipped the rest of the afternoon's sessions to sit on her balcony, eyes closed, listening to the surf, letting the breeze and sun compete against each other to caress her skin, to destress from the day's events. From life.

And to think about Matthew.

"Were you avoiding me?"

She stumbled, but recovered quickly enough that she hoped he hadn't noticed. She had been avoiding him, but she wasn't admitting that.

"Why would I avoid you?" *Because she'd acted foolish.* "I don't know you."

He shook his head. "I thought… Never mind. You're here now." His lips curved. "Let's have an enjoyable evening and remedy you not knowing me by our getting to know each other." Although he was smiling and charming, his face took on that dark and dangerous look that, no doubt, made women fall to their knees to do his bidding, as he added, "A lot better."

Willing her legs to keep her upright, Natalie gulped, accepting that she was powerless to resist his powers, and that, even if she could, she didn't want to. He was a fantasy come to life. Never would she have imagined he'd been looking for her.

She wasn't sure what had changed from his earlier decline of her offer, but now he wasn't attempting to hide his interest, his intent.

Good. Neither was she. Life was too short for silly games.

Getting to know each other better should have been easy enough during the delicious meal since their chairs were next to each other, but there were six other people at the table. Two couples who'd introduced themselves, and two male pediatricians who had gone to medical school together and met up once a year at a continuing medical education conference for old times' sake and a catch-up. All six people vied for Matthew's attention. He included her in the conversation, stopped several times to ask her opinion, but with the others at the table Natalie could barely get a word in edgewise.

Which was okay by her. She sat back, watching and listening in fascination as Matthew discussed his work. Part of her wasn't quite able to believe she sat next to *the* Dr. Matthew Coleman she'd quoted in several of her medical school papers. Another part wasn't able to believe she sat next to the sexiest man she'd ever met. All of her was dazed that both could be the same man, and that when he looked at her his eyes burned with pale blue fire.

Soon after their table had finished the meal, the moderator took the podium and called the room's attention to the front, silencing conversations around the room. Ending his discussion with the two pediatricians, Matthew turned, caught Natalie watching him—probably with a goofy *I want you* expression on her face—and grinned. Dark and dangerous had been right, because that grin threatened all her good sense.

Then again, sitting next to him made perfect sense.

Why wouldn't it? Despite her three-year relationship with Jonathan, they weren't together any more. With his devotion to his career matching hers, he'd easily fit into her life because he didn't mind the large amount of time her job ate up. Or so he'd said, right up to the moment he'd defended his sleeping with another woman by pointing out Natalie's refusal to commit more time to him and marry him.

Fine. Good riddance and thank God she hadn't been willing to marry a man who'd so readily cheat. She wanted marriage, to connect completely with another person, to someday have a family, but something had held her back from saying yes to Jonathan. Maybe it had been that she was still building her dream career.

No matter. Jonathan was history. She was free to do whatever she chose. With whomever she chose.

Her gaze connected with Matthew's.

He leaned close to her ear, giving her a waft of his spicy aftershave. "This hasn't exactly been conducive to getting to know each other."

The man smelled amazing. She wanted to breathe him in and hold her breath for ever.

"Is that what we're doing?" she whispered back, knowing her eyes revealed everything she was feeling in case he'd missed it in her husky voice.

"You want to leave?"

Yes!

"And miss the keynote?"

His lips twitched with amusement. "You want to go first and meet in the lobby in fifteen minutes or shall we leave together?"

Whether it was for her privacy or his, she liked that he was giving her the option to choose to leave together, which implied he didn't mind anyone knowing he was with her, or their leaving separately so no one would be the wiser. It was up to her to decide how they proceeded.

Still, she had a few things to clarify first.

"Are you single?"

Obviously startled at her question, he nodded.

"Then meet me by the fountain in ten." She pushed back her chair and quietly excused herself from the group at their table.

As she weaved her way through the tables to where she could make her escape, Natalie fought kicking up her high heels with joy. She felt good, light, feminine. And, even though she worried about stumbling, she was glad she had on her heels because they plumped her calves and made her legs look toned. She wanted to look good because Matthew's gaze was on her. She could feel it as surely as if his hands traced over her skin.

She made it out the door just before a happy giggle bubbled from her lips. This was crazy. She was behaving like a teenager sneaking out of the house to meet a boyfriend. She was a grown woman sneaking out of a conference keynote to meet an attractive man in the lobby.

Despite her bravado at the idea of a short-term affair with Matthew, she hadn't actually ever *had* an affair. She and Jonathan had dated for several months prior to their having sex, and she'd cared about him. She'd never had any desire for a physical relationship prior to him. She'd been too busy focusing on her studies, her career, determined to make a difference in pediatric cardiology.

Honestly, despite Monica's and Suzie's advice to "get laid" this weekend, she'd had no intention of doing so. Not until she'd seen Matthew at the airport and he'd cast a spell over her mind and body to where she craved him.

Still, what if she couldn't go through with sex for the sake of sex and Matthew got upset?

She hesitated outside the ballroom door.

Stop it, she scolded herself. Just stop over-thinking and go with the flow. Emotional commitment was overrated. Just look at what had happened with her last committed relationship.

Whether it was because of the blow Jonathan's cheating had done to her ego or because she was hundreds of miles from home, or some unknown reason, she wasn't going to let her brain get in the way of her having a good time. Excitement surged through every inch of her body. Excitement that she was doing something outside her comfort zone. Excitement that a sexy man looked at her as if he wanted to yank off her clothes and kiss her all over.

For the next three days she'd let whatever happened between her and Matthew happen, and not dwell on the possibility that after the conference ended it was unlikely she'd ever see him again.

Wasn't that actually perfect? Because she needed to focus on Memphis Children's Hospital and upping their pediatric cardiology department to the next level. To stepping up to the new role the hospital was going to offer her.

She didn't need Matthew, or anyone else, distracting her.

But at the moment she was in Florida at a gorgeous resort hotel and she was going to enjoy the rest of the evening.

With Matthew.

Suzie and Monica would be proud.

Unable to drag his gaze from Natalie's retreating backside, Matthew knew he wasn't fooling a single person in the room. At the moment he didn't care.

He *should* care.

He had a child to think about, so his behavior mattered. He had to set a good example for Carrie.

But Carrie was in Memphis with his mother, as Matthew had signed up for this continuing education conference before he'd known he was going to be raising his god-daughter. He'd started to cancel, but his mother had pushed him not to, saying he needed a weekend to decompress after the past few months. Carrie was better off with his mother than she was with him anyway.

His heart pinched as he thought of Robert and Carolyn. The couple had died much too soon in a small plane crash, leaving their most precious possession to him. Four-year-old Carrie.

What had his best friends been thinking? Although serious in his professional life, he'd been a happy-go-lucky bachelor who knew how to have a good time without the burden of commitment.

Robert had been Matthew's best friend since grammar school. They'd gone through university then med school together. He'd been there when Carolyn had stolen his friend's heart, had been best man at their wedding, had been there for Carrie's birth.

Having been only children to single moms, neither Robert nor Carolyn had had any living family and had asked Matthew to be Carrie's godfather prior to her birth. Not believing he'd ever actually be raising the little girl, Matthew had agreed. Nothing was supposed to have happened to his friends.

But three months ago, it had. Something horrible that neither he nor Carrie would recover from, when the couple's small-engine plane had crashed, instantly killing them both.

If only his friends had made better arrangements for their daughter. Surely anything would have been better than him.

Matthew paused outside the ballroom door. What was he doing? His life was in total upheaval. He should not get involved with Natalie or any other woman when his world was so topsy-turvy.

Wasn't that why he'd hesitated to accept Natalie's invitation to sit beside her?

To let her think there could be anything between them would be wrong. He had a whole new messed-up life he had to figure out. Until he did, Carrie had to be his priority. Only, so long as he made sure Natalie knew that whatever happened in Miami would end in Miami, there was no reason why they couldn't enjoy the next few days. He *needed* the next few days. He'd not had sex in months. Not since before his friends had... Hell, he didn't want to think of that anymore.

Natalie would likely tell him to kiss her lovely behind when he told her he couldn't offer more than a few days of fun in the sun. Sure, there had been a rare moment when he'd been at Robert and Carolyn's that he'd envied their relationship, the closeness they shared. But he had never actively thought about marriage or a long-term relationship for himself. He liked being single, liked being able to do what he wanted when he wanted with whomever he wanted, that if he wanted to stay at the hospital for twenty-four hours straight there was no one to complain or be disappointed that his work meant more than they did.

All that had changed with Carrie. Now, whether he wanted to or not, he had to keep a regular schedule, had to come home at night.

He raked his fingers through his hair. Yeah, he hadn't been free to do much of anything over the past three months. Instead, he'd been trying to figure out what to do with the sweetest little girl he'd ever known, who was heartbroken over the loss of her parents and who had the unfortunate luck of being in Uncle Matthew's care.

Uncle Matthew, who was now thrust into the role of *Daddy* Matthew.

For the next three days he got to just be Matthew, and to do what he wanted.

And what Matthew wanted was Natalie. Naked and beneath him.

There she was, waiting by the fountain, her gaze dancing with seduction and making his head spin. Would it be wrong if he threw her over his shoulder, carried her to his hotel room and took her every way he'd imagined over the course of the day? He couldn't recall ever wanting a woman more than he wanted Natalie. Had to be the turmoil of the past three months and his need to just…escape. That, and the fact he'd not even thought about a woman or sex since Robert and Carolyn's death. His reaction to Natalie was probably his subconscious guiding him to take what he could while he could.

He made his way to the fountain, took Natalie's hand and practically dragged her toward the elevator bank where he'd been waiting for her earlier.

CHAPTER THREE

"I WANT TO make love to you, Natalie," Matthew told her as the elevator doors slid shut behind them.

Natalie's breath caught.

"But—" he began.

No! She didn't want there to be a "but". *Please, the one time she was willing to just let go and have a fling with a man, don't let him have a reason they couldn't.*

With his free hand he pressed the door-close button rather than a floor number, then continued. "I don't want to deceive you in any way, and, if we go further without my telling you the truth, that's what I'd feel I was doing."

Had he lied to her earlier? *Was* there someone special in his life?

Please don't be married or engaged or whatever it is that's so horrible that you have to confess before having sex.

"You're a beautiful, intelligent woman and

deserve better than anything I'm able to give. Which is why I need to explain all the reasons why you should tell me no." He took a deep breath, kept those pale blue eyes locked with hers. "Beyond the next three days, I have nothing to offer to you or any woman."

Natalie's breath caught, at his words and at his hand still clenching hers.

"I don't understand," she admitted, trying to make sense of what he was saying.

"What I've wanted from the moment you stepped off this elevator before dinner was to put you right back on it, go to one of our rooms and not come out for hours."

He watched her as if he half expected her to pull her hand free and slap him.

As if.

"You're not married?"

His look of shock gave answer before his words.

"There's no other woman in my life, Natalie. It's just that my life is complicated, and letting you think there could be anything beyond the next three days would be wrong. Whatever happens between us this weekend ends when we leave Miami on Sunday. When deciding what floor this elevator stops on, keep that in mind."

So neither of them wanted anything beyond the next three days, and time was too precious to waste. She wanted him. He wanted her. They didn't need to know anything more about each other.

Well, almost nothing more.

"Are you…?" How did she ask this? She'd been a virgin with Jonathan and was screened annually at the hospital, so she hadn't had to do blood tests or anything of the sort. Trying to convince her it was time for them to take that next step, he'd gone on his own and given her a copy of his lab tests prior to their becoming physically involved. As time and their busy schedules had allowed, they'd fallen into a mutually satisfying relationship.

Or maybe it hadn't been so mutually satisfying, since he'd been having sex with another woman.

Ugh. No. She was not going to let thoughts of Jonathan's infidelity creep into this moment. All she needed to know was—how did couples usually bring up a clean bill of health? Or did they? No matter what other couples did. She would ask.

"I mean, do you have...?" She struggled to find the right words.

"I'm clean, if that's what you're asking."

Relief filled her at his answer and at how easily he'd known what she was asking.

"Me, too," Natalie assured, excitement coursing through her. Excitement and heat. White-hot heat that burned at her very core. She wanted Matthew. More than she'd ever wanted any man. Mentally and physically. She. Wanted. Him.

She reached for his hand. "We both know what we want, and it isn't a relationship." There. She'd said it. There could be no confusion. "So, truly, your comments, while gentlemanly, are a waste of valuable time when you could be impressing me in ways I'd appreciate much more." Her boldness surprised her, but good grief, he seemed intent on being a gentleman when what she wanted was a rogue lover setting her body on fire. "My room is on the eleventh floor." She reached over and pressed the button. "Are you getting off with me or not?"

Despite her brave invitation, Natalie's hands trembled as she slid her card into the key slot. Her heart pounded as the little green lights flashed and she twisted the handle, opening the door to let Matthew into her hotel room.

Even as her feet moved, carrying her inside, she asked herself how this worked. Did she go to the bathroom and freshen up? Did he? Did she just take off her clothes and get into bed, as Jonathan had always preferred?

Once they were inside the room and she heard him secure the lock, she turned to him, hoping to break the silence that had enveloped them on their ascent to her room.

Before she could get a word out, Matthew pushed her back a couple of steps to sandwich her between the wall and his hard body, his mouth covering hers. There was nothing slow, indecisive or gentlemanly in his touch.

Finally, she thought.

His mouth was ravenous. His hands roaming over her body voracious. His lean hips pressing against her belly giving proclamation of just how much he wanted her.

She kissed him, touched him with equal intensity, running her hands over his arms, his shoulders, cupping his face in her hands as his kiss deepened.

One little kiss and they'd gone straight to fast and furious.

Ha. There was nothing little about how Matthew was kissing her. Big. Huge. Gigantic. That was how his kisses felt.

That was how his body felt grinding against her.

Fireworks went off in her head, in her chest, her whole body, at his mouth moving over hers, at his hands sliding over her, tugging her blouse from her skirt and letting in a swoosh of welcome cool air across her sensitized flesh.

"I can't believe you're here, that we're doing this," she murmured as he traced kisses along her neck, her collarbone. She dug her fingers into his hair.

"You aren't changing your mind, are you?" he breathed against the indentation at her throat, his tongue darting out to dip into the sensitive flesh.

Natalie quivered.

"No. Never." She arched against his mouth. "This is what I have played over and over in my mind today."

What she needed. Crazy, but she *did* need him—this virtual stranger who was setting her body on fire. His touch, his kiss, his full attention. His body grinding against hers, hard, lean, thrilling.

"Tell me what you want, Natalie," he coaxed, pushing her blouse off her shoulders and letting the silky material pool around her red heels, revealing her lacy white camisole and matching bra beneath. Cupping her bottom, he bent, kissing the valley between her breasts. "Tell me what you've been imagining us doing."

"That," she breathed, running her fingers into his thick, inky dark hair and holding him to her breast. "I like that."

That. That. That, her body screamed.

"Me, too." Pushing aside her camisole and bra, he took a puckered nipple into his mouth and gave a gentle tug.

Natalie almost died. Or exploded. Or imploded. Or all of the above, so many sensations shot through her electrified body. His hands held urgency as he continued to caress her, his mouth claiming everything in its passionate path. Within breathless minutes he pushed her skirt up her hips to bunch at her waist so he could slide his hands inside her panties to cup her bottom once more.

Yeah, she wanted that, too.

His hands were hot on her skin, electrifying. She wanted him. Desperately. She kissed him with that desperation. Touched him with that desperation. Moved her body against his with that desperation. Her fingers found their way to his waist, to where he strained against his dress pants' zipper. After a moment's fumbling, she had his pants to where she could touch him. She explored what she craved to feel deep inside.

"Natalie," he groaned. Or maybe he'd growled.

Either way, she'd never heard her name said as Matthew had just said it. Had never felt the power filling her at how he responded to her slightest touch.

"I like this, too," she whispered close to his ear, in awe at how free she felt to touch him, at how uninhibited to give and take as she pleased. She'd never felt this freedom with Jonathan. She had always followed his lead rather than blazing a path of her own. "I like touching you and feeling your reaction and knowing I did that."

He mumbled something against her throat, where his mouth was wreaking havoc on her nervous system, but she didn't catch his words. They didn't matter. His body was telling her all she needed to know.

"I like what you're doing," she continued, barely recognizing her voice, but further emboldened by the fervor of his kisses. "I like the way you're touching me, as if you *need* to touch me." She'd never felt more desirable than in this moment, than the way his touch made her feel. He made her feel beautiful, desirable, wanton even. Unlike anything she'd ever felt or would possibly ever feel again. The knowledge promised ecstasy.

"That makes two of us," he assured her, between more ardent kisses.

"I like the way you're looking at me," she continued, her voice breathy, her fingers tightening around him. "As if you want to put every detail of me to memory."

Matthew didn't have to put every detail of Natalie to memory.

She was already there.

Every delectable inch of her.

He had no doubt he'd never forget what was happening. She was timeless, beautiful. Unforgettable.

Barely hanging on to his sanity, he took her hands into his, kissed her fingertips, then pressed against her. Eyes locked with his, her fingers moved to his shoulders, kneaded deep into his muscles as he grazed her lips with his teeth.

"More," she breathed, arching into his touch. "I want more."

Completely caught between him and the wall, she shifted her hips against him, pressing her upper body against the wall to give added pressure to the sensuous contact between their bodies.

A long leg slid up his, wrapped itself around his waist, pressing her pelvis more fully against where he throbbed.

Heaven help him.

They were barely inside her hotel room door and he was about to rip off her panties and take her like a madman. He'd meant to take her slow, to kiss her all over, and when she was ready, take them both over the edge.

Her body was ready now.

He could feel her damp heat burning into him and that reality undid every good intention he had of *slow*. Her mouth was against his now, hard and demanding. Her hands tugged at his shirt, managing to pull the material loose. He wasn't sure if she'd unbuttoned it or popped every button. It didn't matter. All that mattered was having her.

She made him manic, illogical, driven by physical need in ways he didn't understand.

"Now," she urged, her fingernails raking over his back, then gripping his buttocks to pull him tighter against her. "I want you inside me now."

Matthew didn't need to be told twice. Supporting her weight between his body and the wall, he reached into his sagging back pocket for his wallet, pulling out a condom.

"I only have one of these," he confessed, ripping it open and making haste of putting it on. "I have the feeling I'm going to wish I had a dozen more before morning."

Her eyes molten honey, Natalie kissed his mouth, hard, full of passion, and, keeping her eyes locked with his, she guided him to his own personal heaven.

Natalie's boldness shocked her. Her boldness in how she touched Matthew, in how she wrapped both legs around his waist and took him deep inside her body with her skirt bunched at her waist and her panties pushed aside.

Her boldness in the things she said to him, in how vocal she was about what she wanted from him and to do to him.

Even more, she was shocked by how she bit down on his shoulder to keep from crying out as an orgasm rocked her body at his powerful thrusts.

Wave after wave of pleasure ripped through her.

If not for the wall, his strong body against hers, she'd have dropped to the floor to float her way back to the land of mere mortal beings.

She thought he'd climaxed with her, but he must have somehow held back. Rather than relax against her as she'd expected, he kept moving, pounding against her as she peaked in pleasure, then started the cataclysmic climb all over again, leaving her frantically moving against him until she went places she'd never been, to heights she'd never scaled, until she went into a blissful free fall that might go on for days.

Weeks.

Just when her orgasm began to spiral out of control, his willpower broke and her body became unwound with him, every nerve cell inside her zinging to life and exploding with a heated force so amazing she couldn't believe her body remained intact.

Intact? More like turned inside out and back again.

From her biased, soaring view, this man lost in passion was a glorious thing.

A satisfied Matthew's damp forehead dropping to rest against hers as he stared into her eyes was splendid. The way her body felt was beautiful. *Everything* felt so beautiful that Natalie wondered if orgasms were mind-altering.

Her mind had definitely been altered.

"If I'd known this was how it would be, we'd have never made it off the elevator."

Looking a bit mind-altered himself, Matthew laughed. "You might be right."

"Might be?" She squeezed her thighs, loving how his eyes darkened instantly in response. He kissed her forehead, and when his gaze met hers there was a contentment in his eyes that puffed up her chest.

She smiled at him with a confidence she didn't understand, but that felt addictive. Yeah, they'd had amazing sex. This was the after part. Shouldn't she feel awkward? Embarrassed by her daring?

She didn't. She felt... She searched for a way to describe what she felt. More connected with him than with any person she'd ever known. How could she feel that way with someone she'd just met? Much freer than she'd ever been with

Jonathan. She'd enjoyed their sex life, but, compared to what she had just experienced, sex with Jonathan had been boring. And not only because she'd just been pushed up against a wall still half-dressed and ravaged, rather than in bed with calm, intentional acts meant to please.

The way her body had responded was what had been different.

Matthew electrified every nerve ending, making her aware of every cell, every nuance of her body, of his body. She'd never had orgasms like those she'd just experienced. Maybe no woman had ever experienced orgasms like the ones Matthew had just given to her.

Whether it was how she'd admired his mind for years or how his sex appeal had toyed with her psyche from the moment she'd laid eyes on him, everything about this moment felt right. Perfect. For that, she hugged him.

His forehead still against hers, his breathing ragged, he searched her eyes. "What was that for?"

"A token of my appreciation." Legs feeling a little shaky, she lowered them from his waist to tentatively support her weight. She felt so languid, she might collapse on the floor.

"I'm the one who needs to be expressing my

gratitude, and my apologies for not hauling your delectable body up here the moment that first workshop finished."

"No worries. I have every intention of giving you lots of opportunity to express your, um, gratitude." Her tone was flirty and it felt good. "And to let you make up for wasting time."

Had she ever flirted with a man before?

She'd always been focused on school, on her patients, her research, her career. Focusing on a man hadn't ever been a priority. But she liked flirting with Matthew, liked the quick smile that transformed his handsome face.

Reaching for her skirt, she tugged the wrinkled material down her hips, then pressed a quick kiss to his lips. Aware that his gaze tracked her every move, she walked to the mini-fridge, took out a bottled water, twisted off the lid and took a drink.

"Thirsty?" She offered the bottle.

He took a long swig, then handed it back to her. "Not now."

His tone implied it hadn't been the water that had quenched his thirst.

Eyeing him, Natalie placed her lips over where his had been and took another drink, letting the water cool her throat.

"Thank you, Natalie."

"For?"

"You know." Winking at her, he went to the bathroom, she assumed to dispose of the used condom, then returned to the room with his pants restored.

That was when she got her first real look at his chest and abdomen. Earlier, she'd been distracted with need and sex, and had been up close to his body, but now... *Oh, my.*

Matthew without a shirt was a beautiful sight.

She'd touched that chest, kissed that chest, been pressed up against that chest, all hot and sweaty.

Feeling quite smug that she'd just had sex with the hottest man alive, she couldn't help but smile. "Now what?"

He shrugged. "Not any more of that, unless we make a protection run, I'm sad to say."

She eyed him curiously. She'd not really considered that they could have a repeat that night. Jonathan had never more than once... *Oh, forget Jonathan.* "Would you really be able to do that again?"

"Just say the word."

Surely he was exaggerating, but his answer still stroked her ego. She knew she shouldn't keep comparing what had just happened to her relationship with her ex, but he'd have rolled over and been asleep already.

Then again, she would have been, too.

Intrigued, and more than a little smug, she asked, "If I said now, you'd want to again tonight?"

He arched a brow. "You have to ask after what we just did? Of course I want to do that again."

"One box isn't enough. Buy two."

Matthew grinned at the woman tugging at his arm and grabbed another box off the shelf. "Two boxes for three nights? You trying to kill me?"

"You're the one who bragged you were able to repeat the deed anytime I said the word," she reminded with a saucy flash of her eyes.

Wondering why he'd ever hesitated in allowing himself this three-day break from reality, Matthew laughed. "You saying the word? If so, I'm sure we can find a vacant corridor."

Her eyes widened momentarily, but she quickly looked intrigued. So much for his prim and proper impression of her at the airport. Thank God he'd given himself permission to forget the real world and just play for three days. Three days to spend with this surprising woman.

Chuckling, he grabbed her hand. "Come on, Natalie. Let's go pay for our two boxes."

They'd opted to walk the beach to a neighboring hotel's gift shop rather than risk one of their colleagues seeing them stock up at the conference hotel. Matthew had enjoyed the sea air and having Natalie's hand clasped within his during the nighttime walk, but the fifteen minutes back to their hotel suddenly seemed like a long time.

"How did you get involved with the Libertine robot project?" she asked once they were back on the beach and headed toward their hotel.

"You want to talk shop?" He just wanted to get back to the hotel and get her naked. Completely this time. He had a lot of exploring to do and was looking forward to discovering every nook and cranny.

"The Libertine fascinates me," she continued, her hand snug in his. "I've watched you perform surgery with it, you know."

He shot a look at her, the moonlight casting just enough light across her face to illuminate her beautiful features. "No, I didn't know."

"I couldn't tell much about you, since you were wearing a surgical mask, glasses and cap and the film clip pretty much only showed the surgery. I guess technically I watched a video of your hands doing miraculous things, because I don't recall anything of your face and I wouldn't have forgotten your eyes had I ever seen them." She smiled sheepishly, then went on. "From how long I've been seeing your name quoted in the cardiology world, I had thought you much older."

He got that a lot. He'd been fortunate to become involved with the Libertine from early in its inception as a surgical tool. Near the end of med school, his passion had shifted his interest to surgical advances being made in treating congenital defects in utero. Robert had followed suit.

Working for a robotics company, Carolyn had been one of the key design engineers on the Libertine. It was how they'd all met. He and Robert had been practically inseparable since grade school. Carolyn had changed that somewhat, but Matthew had felt more as if they'd added a third player to their team, rather than their friendship losing anything, when his best friend married the brilliant engineer.

He missed them so much. Three months and it didn't seem real that he'd never see them again, never discuss the Libertine, or difficult cases. Never catch another football game while Carolyn laughed at their long-term rivalry of the Cowboys against the Steelers. Never again—

"You okay?" Natalie's voice broke into Matthew's memories.

Fighting back the hollow ache in his gut, he clenched his teeth. How had he let such depressing thoughts in tonight when he felt alive, truly alive, for the first time since before he'd gotten the call that Robert and Carolyn's plane had gone down?

"Just got lost in thought." He flashed a smile that wasn't as real as he'd like, but there wasn't enough light that she'd likely be able to tell. "How old do you think I am?"

She glanced his way a few moments, making him wonder if perhaps she saw better in the low light than he'd given her credit for, but she seemed to make the decision not to push. Maybe because she didn't want to know what he'd really been thinking about.

"Uh-uh." Her smile was wide, bright, not so over-the-top as to come across as completely fake. "I'm not guessing your age. If I go too high you might be offended. If I go too low, you'll accuse me of robbing the cradle."

Her voice was light, but her grip on his hand had tightened, offering a comfort he soaked up and was amazed at how much better her smile and touch left him feeling.

He chuckled. "No chance you robbed the cradle, Natalie. That would be me. I'm probably a good ten years older than you."

"I seriously doubt it." She told him her age.

"Eight years older," he corrected. "I'm the one who robbed the cradle, it seems."

"Eight years isn't that much," she assured. "You're barely into your forties."

A memory of his fortieth birthday, spent with Robert and Carolyn, popped into his head. They'd rented out their favorite restaurant's back room, invited a ton of mutual friends and acquaintances and surprised him with a birthday bash.

"Hey—you okay?" she asked again.

Why had his friends popped back into his head so quickly when he'd just scolded himself for letting them in on a night meant to drown them out?

His gaze cut to Natalie. Why did he find himself wanting to tell her about them?

"You quit walking," she pointed out. "And

you're squeezing my hand as if you're afraid if you let go the wind might carry me out to sea."

Matthew forced his fingers to pry loose from hers, raked them through his hair. "Sorry."

"That sensitive about your age, huh? I'll keep that in mind and be sure not to make any more age references."

Pushing thoughts of his friends from his mind yet again, Matthew shook his head and gave in to Natalie's teasing. "I've no problem with being called an old man."

"Old man?" Natalie laughed, took his hand back into hers and gave him a little squeeze. "You aren't an old man. Admittedly, it's a bit kinky, but I'd be happy to oblige if that's what you want me to call you."

His smile was real. "As long as you're calling me, I won't complain."

Her gaze searched his. "For the rest of the weekend, right?"

"Right," Matthew agreed, but suddenly found it difficult to keep his smile in place. "For the next three days, I'm all yours."

Then he'd fly back to Memphis, stay at his mother's for a night, then he and Carrie would drive back to Boston because the little girl was terrified of the thought of getting on a plane, and he hadn't forced the issue.

Back to trying to figure out life without Robert and Carolyn.

Back to him struggling to raise their precious daughter in a way that wouldn't disappoint them, which seemed impossible for a sworn bachelor who still couldn't even put Carrie's hair up without missing handfuls of it from the bun.

Too bad the position in Memphis hadn't worked out so his family would be close to shower Carrie in their love and guide him in the right direction as he got this parenting thing all wrong time and again.

What did he know about raising a kid?

Nothing. His friends had been foolish leaving Carrie's upbringing to him. Robert had known Matthew had no plans to marry or have children. Truly, they couldn't have chosen a worse guardian for Carrie.

"Your hand is getting tight again," Natalie warned.

He loosened his hold. "Sorry."

"Want to talk about whatever keeps bothering you?"

He couldn't blame Natalie for asking. She'd

let it go more than once, but he kept going back to places he didn't need to let his brain go.

"It's not important." Which was a lie. Everything about Robert and Carolyn was important. How he was going to handle fatherhood was important. Part of him wanted to tell Natalie, to spill everything out to her, to tell her what a screw-up step-in parent he'd been so far and that he wished he could give Carrie to a couple who knew what they were doing so the kid wouldn't turn out messed up. But losing his best friends, and his failed parenthood, weren't decent conversation for a three-day affair.

For the next three days, he was just Matthew. The dedicated heart surgeon and researcher, the fun-loving man, the devoted short-term lover.

CHAPTER FOUR

NATALIE MADE IT to breakfast just before the hotel wait staff cleared the buffet trays.

Having gone earlier to his hotel room to shower, Matthew had arrived before her and was at a table with two other men and a woman, eating breakfast. Wearing his khaki pants and blue button-up shirt with the sleeves folded to mid-forearm, a smile on his handsome face, he stole her breath.

She could hardly believe she'd had sex with him. Hot, needy, carnal sex.

Natalie lingered, overfilling her plate with sliced fruit. There was no reason she couldn't join Matthew and the others at his table, but she procrastinated, toying with toasting a slice of wheat bread.

She'd seen and touched every part of his body. With her hands, her mouth. They'd done things that just recalling was enough to make her blush and wonder who that wanton woman in bed with him had been. After all that, was she really hesitating to sit down beside him to eat breakfast?

When she'd finally gotten her plate and headed in his direction, Matthew rose from his chair.

"There's a seat at our table, Natalie. Join us."

He'd made it easy. As if he were inviting an old friend or colleague to join his table. No big deal. Only, when their gazes met, his unusual eyes held a warmth that conveyed that his smile was for her alone. Nothing had changed from the time he'd left her room. He had no morning-after regrets.

Her gaze dropped to his mouth, and she fought the urge to lean over and plant another good-morning kiss on his magic lips.

Those lips had kissed her all over. More than once. Places she'd never been so thoroughly kissed. Those hands had held her, touched her, coaxed responses she'd not known her body able to give.

Natalie gulped back the emotion looking at him filled her with. Pride, pleasure, passion. Maybe they should skip the conference and go back to her room? No, they'd decided they would both attend morning classes to earn their continuing-education credits. As much as she'd like to drag him back to her room, she'd restrain herself.

At least until morning break.

A little giddy at the thought, she smiled at the others as she joined the table.

"Natalie, this is Dr. Kim Yang, Dr. Steven Powers and Dr. Herb Fallows. They all practice pediatrics at Loma Linda in California."

She set her plate on the table and shook the outstretched hands as Matthew continued the introductions.

"And this talented lady is Dr. Natalie Sterling."

She'd swear she saw him wink at her from the corner of her eye, but she kept her focus on the others.

"Natalie is a pediatric cardiac surgeon at Memphis Children's Hospital with Dr. Ramone Luiz," he continued.

"Hi." Smiling, she sat down and turned to ask Matthew something that had been nagging at her mind and hit her again when he mentioned the hospital. "I've been meaning to ask you— why did *you* fly in from Memphis?"

For the briefest moment his face took on the dark expression he'd had on the plane, but it

quickly disappeared behind a smile. "I was visiting family."

Reminding herself not to sound too personal
in front of the others, she asked, "You have family in Memphis?"

Asking personal questions probably wasn't
a good idea when a woman was only having
a three-day affair, but she hadn't been able to
curb her curiosity.

He hesitated a moment. "My mother lives just
over the Hernando de Soto Bridge on the Arkansas side."

Natalie's pulse pounded at her temple. She
lived on Mud Island. His mother lived just
across the Mississippi River from her. That
meant he probably came to Memphis from time
to time to visit.

Natalie put a hold on her racing thoughts of
possibly seeing him again in the future.

Three days. That was what they'd agreed to
and what she'd stick to. They were only on Friday of their weekend together. They still had the
rest of the day, all of Saturday and part of Sunday before she flew home. It would be enough.

Even if by some miracle Matthew wanted to
continue to see her, trying to maintain a long-
distance relationship would be near impossi-

ble. She already worked long hours. When she got her promotion she'd be working even longer ones, because she'd essentially continue to do her job but be taking over the parts of Dr. Luiz's job he was relinquishing with his partial retirement.

If Matthew wanted to see her during his trips to Memphis, she'd say no. Sticking to the three days would be better than trying to stretch out what couldn't last and turning a fantasy into something waiting to fall apart.

"West Memphis in Arkansas isn't that far from where I live," she said, feeling as if she should say something for the benefit of the other three at the table, who were listening in curiously.

Maybe for Matthew, too, as he'd become overly interested in his food.

If he thought he needed to worry that she would push to see him in Tennessee, he was wrong. She had her priorities, and a relationship beyond Sunday was not one of them, no matter how phenomenal a lover he was.

Fortunately, the conversation turned to the conference. A few minutes later, the two men left the table, but Dr. Yang stayed and chatted with Matthew and Natalie about everything from her vegan diet to her faith.

The room had cleared out except for the wait staff cleaning the room.

"I've kept you two from making it to the first session on time," Kim said, glancing at her fitness wristband and wincing when she realized what time it was. "Sorry."

"No problem," Natalie assured, placing her fork and napkin on her empty plate. "I was late coming downstairs anyway."

Not really late, but when she and Matthew had calculated how long they could stay in bed that morning they'd not allotted time for mealtime socializing.

"Maybe we can sneak into the back and catch the presentation highlights."

When they rose to leave the table, Kim swayed.

Natalie noted how pale she was and moved around the table. "Are you okay?"

But she was too late. Kim's eyes rolled back and her knees buckled, causing her to slump backward. Just before she hit the carpeted floor, Matthew grasped the woman, lowering her to the carpet.

"Dr Yang?" He gently shook her. "Can you hear me?"

Natalie checked the woman's pulse, normal at seventy-six beats per minute. Although unconscious, she was breathing okay, too. "Vitals are stable."

Pulling a chair to Dr. Yang, Matthew propped her feet in the chair to cause increased blood flow to her vital organs anyway.

"Is she okay?" one of the waiters asked, stooping beside them at the commotion of Dr. Yang losing consciousness. "Do I need to call 911?"

Natalie started to say yes, but Dr. Yang's eyelids fluttered and she grabbed hold of Natalie's arm.

"No ambulance," she muttered, so low Natalie strained to know what she'd said.

Further concern filled Natalie. "You're sure? You passed out. At the minimal, you need labs."

The woman shook her head. "Not sick." Her hand lowered to her belly and she weakly smiled. "Just pregnant."

Natalie's eyes widened and she stared at the woman in surprise. "Oh."

"Congratulations," Matthew said from where he knelt next to them, but Natalie couldn't tell if he meant the word or not.

"I'll call for an ambulance if you think I need to." The waiter looked to Natalie for instruction.

She eyed the pale woman, whose color was slowly returning. "You sure you're okay?"

Kim scooted onto her elbows and paused. "I will be when this nine-month deal is up. I've heard of morning sickness, but this light-headedness is ridiculous."

"Is your obstetrician aware you're having light-headedness?" Matthew looked ready to catch the woman if she so much as wobbled.

Kim nodded and gave a heartfelt sigh. "He thinks I need to suck it up. Don't I know that other women work right up until birth, plop that baby out, then go right back to working?"

Horrified, Natalie stared at the woman, who had now maneuvered herself into a sitting position with her legs down off the chair.

"Let me guess," Matthew ventured, understanding dawning. "Your obstetrician is your husband?"

Kim smiled. "Bingo. He's a wonderful man, a wonderful obstetrician, but is struggling with empathy for his wife."

"Sounds like you need a new obstetrician," Natalie recommended, struggling with empathy for the man.

Kim shook her head. "Lee is going to deliver our baby at home. It's what we both want. I can't imagine anyone other than him delivering our child."

Kim braced her palms against the floor and pushed herself, slowly standing. She stood still a moment, testing the waters, then smiled. "I shouldn't have made him sound such a tyrant. Pregnancy hormones and these waves of dizziness have made me cranky."

Both Matthew and the waiter moved alongside Kim as she sat back at the table.

"I'm fine. I've kept you two from the conference long enough." She glanced at the waiter's name tag and smiled at him. "Jack's going to get me a glass of orange juice, and when I've finished it I'll catch the next presentation."

Natalie felt guilty leaving Dr. Yang, and advised the waiter to call for help if needed, but they did go slip into the presentation. They were twenty minutes late, and a few heads turned when they slid into their seats. Natalie didn't care. There were worse things in life than being associated with a man you had admired from afar for years, and had fallen into immediate lust with upon meeting.

Natalie and Matthew stayed through all the

morning sessions and logged in their continuing education hours. Lunch was sponsored by a pharmaceutical company that manufactured immunizations.

"I'd like to attend the presentation given by Dr. Fielding on in-utero cleft palate repair this afternoon, but perhaps you'd like us to get lunch on our own?" Matthew offered as they reviewed the conference itinerary.

Natalie's gaze lifted and fires danced in the honeyed depths of her eyes. "You mean, on our own as in Room Service?"

He laughed. "I actually meant us meeting in the lobby and renting bikes to ride up the boardwalk to a place I know that has some killer seafood."

Her face was so expressive it was easy to watch her surprise that he didn't immediately take up her offer. Part of him wanted to do just as she'd suggested, but he also wanted to take her for some sunshine, rest and relaxation. He had the feeling she worked too hard.

Had the feeling?

Dr Luiz had gone on and on about her. Natalie deserved the promotion she'd soon be getting. In that regard, Matthew was glad the hospital hadn't met his terms. Natalie would probably have been devastated if had he gotten the job.

"Obviously, you learned nothing from last night." She gave an exaggerated sigh. "But, since I have to eat, I'll meet you in the lobby in twenty minutes," she promised. "But if I have to get on a bicycle for the first time in a zillion years, the food better be as good as you say, and I'm adding this to the list of things you need to make up to me later."

He chuckled. "Noted—and I'll make the wait worth your while."

Natalie had always heard the expression that doing something one had once been proficient at was like riding a bike. Once you knew how, you could just jump right back on.

She'd jumped right back on, but would be lying if she claimed proficiency. She had ridden a bicycle as a child, again when in undergrad and traveling to and from her apartment to campus. That had been several years ago, and her confidence that her bicycle wasn't going to topple over was now lacking.

Or maybe it was that she got the impression Matthew was holding back to stay close to her, that he was trying to keep up a conversation between them, and she needed to focus on what she was doing so her bicycle didn't go careening into his.

Plus, her bottom hurt on the narrow seat.

"Smile, Natalie."

As she parked her bicycle and secured a cord around the frame and locked it in place, she gritted her teeth in a semblance of a smile.

Matthew laughed. "You can do better than that."

"Ask me again when my belly is full."

"Deal." Having secured his own bicycle, he took her hand and they made their way up the wooden deck leading into the restaurant. Although it was busy, the hostess guided them to a table on one of the patios that overlooked the beach.

"Sitting outdoors okay?"

"This is fabulous." She loved the ocean, loved the feel of the breeze on her face, and the patio was covered, had an overhead fan going and offered just the right amount of shade from the hot sun. "Perfect," she added as she sat in a chair and grabbed a menu.

A waitress came by, took their drink order, and Matthew ordered an appetizer to share.

"I could have been allergic to shrimp, you know," she teased when the waitress had left.

"Are you? I can catch her and change the order."

She tried, but couldn't keep a straight face. "No."

"I didn't think so."

Curious, she asked, "Why not?"

He shrugged. "I get the impression you're a woman who has no trouble letting a man know what she wants, doesn't want," his eyes bored into hers, "or what she's allergic to."

She supposed she had given him that impression. With him, telling him, showing him what she wanted had been easy. Maybe because she knew their time was limited and there was a freedom in the knowledge that she'd never see him again afterwards.

Only, his mother was practically her neighbor, so it was possible. Why did that make her heart race?

"Right now," she began, "this woman is going to wash her hands and check to see if I sweated my mascara down my cheeks during that bicycle ride."

"No worries. You are beautiful."

He made her *feel* beautiful, and not just because he'd told her several times that day. Smiling, she winked at him. "If you get lonely before

I get back, you can always sneak into the ladies' room and we could..."

He threw his head back and laughed. "You have a one-track mind."

She did. Pediatric cardiology.

Although for the past twenty-four hours she'd only thought of Matthew.

Probably because he was a renowned heart surgeon.

Or because he was gorgeously fascinating.

One or the other, but either way she was on vacation—sort of—so focusing on something besides work wasn't a crime.

A weekend with Natalie Sterling was like being at a sexual boot camp. One that tested Matthew's stamina and shocked him at how far she pushed him physically. Possibly because he knew this would be his last "free" weekend for a long, long time as he forced himself to settle into his role as Carrie's parent.

Which implied that any woman would do.

Matthew didn't buy it.

The woman lying next to him in her hotel room bed trying to catch her breath drove his body crazy, had his libido, his endurance pushed to unreal heights.

Despite his own heaving chest, he rolled onto his side, planted a kiss on her damp cheek. "That was amazing."

Smiling with that sexy, full mouth of hers, she lowered her lashes in a saucy flutter. "I thought you could do better."

He burst out laughing. "You think?"

"Life goals, Matthew," she said, and tsked, rolling to face him. "Life goals."

"Guess I better get started." He traced his finger over the curve of her bare hip.

Still a little breathless, her eyes widened. "We just…now?"

His finger made figure eights, moving closer and closer to the apex of her legs with each completion. "No time like the present. Besides, I still have to make it up to you for making you ride that bicycle instead of…"

"There is that," Natalie agreed, moving into his touch. "Guess you're right. Might take a lot to make that up to me, considering how I toppled over on the ride home."

Recalling how his insides had felt watching Natalie's front bike wheel running off the edge of the sidewalk, her losing balance and toppling over right into traffic, Matthew stilled the tracing of his hands and rolled over onto her instead. "You okay?"

"I could be better," she said, staring up at him with a challenge in her eyes and the need to be kissed on her lips.

"I'm beginning to think you're just using me for sex, Dr. Sterling," he teased.

Only, if he was just teasing, why did the truth in his words sting? Why did he want to hear Natalie deny that that was what she was doing?

"That's exactly what we're *both* doing, Dr. Coleman," she reminded, her expression guarded. "Now, didn't you mention something about making that bicycle ride up to me?"

CHAPTER FIVE

WITHOUT ANY DIFFICULTY, Matthew swapped his first-class seat for the seat next to Natalie's coach one.

Natalie had been surprised, but like her, she supposed, he was reluctant for their "three days" to end a moment before it had to.

When the plane landed, they'd go their separate ways.

"Don't."

At his single word, she opened her eyes, glanced at him in question.

"You're thinking about when the plane lands again."

"You're right. Sorry." She squeezed the hand holding hers. "It was a great conference, wasn't it?"

"Best ever."

Her gaze cut to his, knowing her eyes were full of questions, then scolded herself for caring so much at what he'd implied.

Yet, she did care.

She bit the inside of her cheek. "I agree."

"Same time next year?"

Natalie laughed a little nervously. "I wish."

"Me, too," he said.

Natalie's chest tightened. Part of her longed to ask if he was serious. Why *couldn't* they meet up again for a weekend of fun? But logic answered her question even before it could really take hold. To make plans to meet up again implied they had a relationship that would continue. They didn't.

The past three days had been perfect. To continue would be only waiting for him to leave, waiting for him to decide he didn't want any more three-day weekends together. She'd been left several times too many already in her life to set herself up that way.

Sticking to their original plan was the way it had to be.

"Thank you for this past weekend, Matthew. How does this work from here?"

His gaze narrowed. "What do you mean?"

"If we accidentally run into each other. What if at some point we are both at the same place at the same time?" After all, his mother lived in Memphis. Yes, the city was large, but stranger things had happened. "Do we pretend we don't know each other or…?" She let her words trail off.

He considered her question. "Who knows what's going to have changed between now and that time if our paths cross again?" His expression tightened. "You might have met someone and—"

"I won't have," she cut in, wanting to set the record straight. "I've learned my lesson."

His expression darkened. "You mean me? Natalie, I—"

She shook her head and hastened to assure, "No. This weekend was wonderful, and exactly what we agreed upon." She took a deep breath. "It's odd. I feel like we shared so much, that you know everything about me, but in reality you know very little."

"I know how to make you…" he continued in a whisper into her ear, winking at her when he straightened back in his seat.

Natalie blushed. "Yes, you know that." He knew her body well. She wouldn't argue with that. "But what you don't know is that two months ago I found out the man I'd been in a relationship with for the past three years was cheating."

"Idiot."

Matthew's absolute confidence in his assessment of Jonathan made Natalie smile.

"Yes, he was. Is," she corrected. "But the truth of the matter is that he did us both a favor, because we didn't want the same things."

"You lived with him?"

Staring at the travel magazine poking out from the seat pocket in front of her, Natalie nodded. "He moved into my condo apartment just over two years ago."

"Is he still there?"

"Good heavens, no." She closed her eyes, then, realizing how he might take her having done so, she opened them. "He's gone and I'm glad."

Matthew stared at her in ways that made her want to close her eyes again.

"You deserve a life, Natalie."

Did he think she didn't know that? But deserving a life and actually getting that life didn't always mesh up. She wanted someone who wouldn't leave her, who could love her completely, but in reality her career seemed the only aspect of her life she had control over.

Fortunately she loved medicine, and her career had never let her down.

* * *

Suzie gave Natalie an "are you crazy?" look. "You didn't get his cell number or social-media account information or anything?"

After Natalie had arrived at her apartment—her practically empty apartment, thanks to Jonathan clearing out his things and quite a few of Natalie's as well—the television hadn't been able to abate the quietness. She'd called and asked her friends to meet her for a late dinner at their favorite downtown restaurant. Tonight, the partially empty rooms had made her feel claustrophobic, alone, and she'd had to get out of the apartment.

"There was no need to exchange numbers." There hadn't been. "We agreed to only three days and said our goodbyes just outside baggage claims."

They'd kept things simple. Three perfect days and nights.

She had no regrets. Other than that she wondered if she'd made a mistake in telling her best friends about Matthew. They'd obviously seen more than there was, and she needed to set the record straight.

"We're much better to have ended things today than to ruin such a perfect memory."

Both her friends shook their heads.

"At least tell me he kissed you goodbye at the airport," Monica insisted, taking a sip of her drink. "One of those long, sappy goodbye kisses that makes a girl kick her leg up and everyone else stare in envy."

"Come on," Suzie urged. "You can't not tell us if he kissed you goodbye. He didn't shake your hand or something else just as lame, did he? Tell all. Best friends want to know."

Recalling how Matthew had kissed her, Natalie smiled. "He kissed me goodbye better than any heroine has ever been kissed goodbye in any romantic movie. Way better."

He had. A kiss that had been full of so much more than just passion. There had been emotion. *Gratitude*, she assured herself. They'd both been thankful for a fun weekend. A very fun weekend. Without meaning to, Natalie added with a sigh, "A goodbye kiss for the ages."

Monica and Suzie exchanged looks, then Monica leaned across the table, wide-eyed, and gasped, "I can't believe it. You fell for this guy."

"No, I didn't," Natalie immediately denied. "He was just…" How could she describe Matthew and how he'd made her feel? "Good, that's all."

"Right. I never saw you all flush-cheeked and starry-eyed when talking about *he whose name we don't say*."

Which was how her friends referred to her ex.

"There's a reason for that. *Jonathan*," she stressed his name, "never did the things to my body that Matthew did. Not even close."

Her friends exchanged looks again, making Natalie feel defensive.

"I had a great weekend, something the two of you encouraged me to do," she reminded. "Why are you acting as if it's a big deal?"

"Why are you?" Suzie pointed out at the same time as Monica said,

"Because it is a big deal. You shouldn't have let him go."

Natalie rolled her eyes. When she'd called her friends, this wasn't what she'd had in mind.

"You both told me to have a holiday fling and I did. An amazing one with a man whose brain is pure genius and whose body should be on a pin-up calendar." She could fan her face just at the memory of his hotness. "I thought you would be proud that I'd done something so out of character."

Her friends just stared.

"Be happy for me," she ordered, getting frustrated with how they kept looking at her.

"We *are* happy for you," Suzie insisted, her big green eyes cutting to Monica for back-up. "Only..."

"Only what?"

"What if this guy was the one?"

Natalie laughed at the absurdity of her friend's question. "He wasn't. It's unlikely I'll ever see him again."

Why did that thought make her insides ache?

"Unlikely?" Suzie piped up. "Does that mean it's possible?"

"Anything is possible. His mother lives in West Memphis and he and I are both pediatric heart surgeons interested in innovative in-utero surgical techniques." Natalie shrugged. "But I don't have plans to intentionally see him again, if that's what you mean."

"Hey, Natalie," Suzie said, her expression one full of glee. "You said you don't mean to intentionally see him again, not that you didn't *want* to see him again."

Yeah, she realized that.

Life without ever setting eyes on Matthew Coleman seemed a long, hard sentence—but why pretend it could be something more?

"So, he's a pediatric heart surgeon." Monica waved a manicured hand. "It can't be that difficult to track down a number to reach him."

No, it wouldn't be. But Natalie wouldn't be tracking him down.

"I won't lie and say there isn't a part of me that would like to see Matthew again, but it's best this way."

Her friends looked doubtful. "What way?"

"With him being a wonderful memory. I've got my career to think about." It was true. With Dr. Luiz's upcoming partial retirement, she did need to focus on her career, not long for things that she'd never had and quite possibly never would. People didn't stick around in her life. Not her parents. Not her foster parents. Not Jonathan.

Not Matthew—but at least she'd known upfront he'd only be in her life for three short days.

Monica rolled her eyes.

Suzie shook her head.

"The hospital board should offer the new position within the next few weeks and I'm going to be busy, busy, busy." She sure hoped so. She needed busy. "I don't need any distractions from what really matters."

"We're not convinced that promotion's a good

thing if it means you're going to be working even more."

Maybe her friends weren't, but Natalie knew better. Heading the cardiology unit when Dr. Luiz stepped back was what she'd dreamed of long before a dark-haired, pale-blue-eyed, beautiful man had completely possessed her mind and body.

Two weeks later, Matthew pulled the phone away from his ear and stared at the device in disbelief. He couldn't have heard right.

Apparently, Carrie's fever had gotten to him and he was now hallucinating. Or maybe it was the lack of sleep over the past thirty-six hours as he'd sat up with her most of the night, afraid to sleep in case her illness worsened—in case he did something else wrong and Carrie paid the price. For the same reasons, he'd called out of work that morning. Something he'd hated to do, but Carrie's preschool wouldn't allow her to go in with a fever and he hadn't had a sick back-up plan short of bringing her to the hospital with him. A feverish child on a neonatal cardiac unit wasn't a good idea under any circumstances, even if it had meant shuffling his entire schedule.

Glancing down at the sleeping little girl's

flushed cheeks and limp body in his lap, he blamed himself for her illness. No doubt he'd messed up somehow. The pediatrician had assured him that she had a normal childhood illness that would pass, that he just needed to keep her hydrated and keep her fever down, but Matthew knew he'd been distracted, had been working long hours where Carrie had been dragged to the hospital repeatedly to make rounds with him. She'd probably picked up something in the hospital hallway.

"The hospital decided having you at Memphis Children's was worth making a few concessions," Dr. Luiz continued on the phone, sounding quite proud of the board's decision. "They're prepared to meet your conditions. All you have to do is say yes and their lawyers will draw up the contract."

Matthew's head spun. "You're serious?"

He and Carrie would be close to his mother and sister, to his family. He'd have help. Carrie would be in the care of people who knew how to care for a child.

Natalie was also there.

A wave of heat flushed his body, making him question again if Carrie's fever had overtaken him, too.

"What about Dr. Sterling? You mentioned her several times when I was in Memphis." Did Natalie know he might be taking the job she wanted? "How does she feel about this?"

"I don't foresee it as being a problem. During their reconciliation of your terms, the board plans for Dr. Sterling to directly work with you."

Matthew wasn't so confident. "She knows, then?"

"Not yet."

Which explained Dr. Luiz's comment about not seeing it as a problem. Matthew knew better, and so would Dr. Luiz soon enough.

"That's the one stipulation to your contract, by the way."

Carrie stirred in her sleep and Matthew stroked his fingers over her back in a soothing manner, waiting for Dr. Luiz's next words, already knowing what the man was going to say.

"With the lighter workload you insisted upon, Dr. Sterling is to share some of the responsibilities that were originally exclusive to your new title. Dr. Sterling is a valued member of our staff. She's excited about the upcoming projects the hospital is involved in. We see her sharing some of the leadership roles at the hospital as the perfect solution to your demands, as well as her continued role at the hospital. We don't want to lose her."

No, he imagined not. Natalie's resume was impressive.

"She will be a great asset to your work at Memphis Children's," Dr. Luiz continued. "You'll be lucky to have her on your team."

No doubt, but she wasn't going to be happy.

Nor was the hospital in Boston, his research team, his office staff.

If he accepted the position in Memphis he'd miss his life in Boston. He *already* missed his life in Boston. He'd had a great life—a booming career, loyal friends, good times and a plethora of women to fill his nights.

His gaze dropped to the child in his arms. Everything had changed, and not for the good. He didn't resent Carrie—he *loved* the kid— but he knew he wasn't cut out for raising a little girl, knew he longed for the freedom he'd known just a few months ago, knew she'd be better off elsewhere. His mother, his sister, his extended family were all in Memphis. People whom he trusted to do what was best for Carrie. As much as the thought of leaving the job he loved in Boston stung, what Dr. Luiz offered was exactly what Carrie needed.

If he said yes, he would be hurting Natalie, would be snatching away something she desperately wanted and, in many ways, deserved. She wasn't likely to forgive him.

Glancing down again at the sick child in his arms, feeling his overwhelming inadequacy in solely providing her care, Matthew admitted that being near his family would be a godsend. His parenting skills weren't up to par, and so far his live-in nanny interviews hadn't turned up a single applicant he trusted.

Had he been in Memphis he wouldn't have had to call out of work today, wouldn't have had to reschedule multiple surgeries that weren't easily rescheduled, because he would have had family willing and able to help. How many more times over Carrie's childhood would she be ill, have needs that would require an unexpected change to their normal routine?

He liked to think he'd been an awesome uncle, but what did he know about being a dad? About meeting the emotional needs of a four-year-old who had lost everyone except him?

Nothing.

Accepting the position in Memphis was a necessity.

* * *

"You're quiet," Dr. Luiz pointed out from across his desk.

Having gotten lost in his thoughts that he'd soon come face to face with a woman he'd thought about way too often over the past month, Matthew leaned back in his chair and shrugged. "It's been a long day."

It had been a long month. More like a long four months, during which his best friends had died and fatherhood had been thrust upon him, ready or not.

"But a good one. This move is good for Memphis Children's, and from what you've told me about your situation it's good for you, too. A win-win for all."

It was a win-win all the way around.

"Except for Dr. Sterling."

Despite the fact that she was technically being promoted, *she* wouldn't think she was a winner. Not when she'd thought she'd be running the whole shebang.

Would she agree to work with him?

If she didn't, if she opted to leave the hospital, perhaps it would be best. He had enough issues to deal with without adding in a sexual attraction to his new co-worker.

Dr Luiz and the board had been all too willing to go along with nothing being said, that the whole deal be kept quiet until Matthew arrived. He'd made the request due to the concerns of his Boston colleagues regarding his research, that he needed to have things settled prior to any word leaking out of his relocation. Boston's work would continue on developing the robot. Matthew had made sure of it.

Working in collaboration with the Boston team, he'd establish a smaller second team in Memphis, one that would implement use of the robot in its upcoming further expansion into in utero heart surgeries. With Memphis Children's eager to expand their pediatric cardiology department's capabilities, the timing couldn't be more perfect.

"Natalie wants what is right for her patients. You being here is for the better of all."

She'd likely hate him. He had enough personal turmoil. He could do without discord at work.

"She is an ambitious woman who has career goals. She wouldn't be human if she didn't resent my having taken what she thought was going to be entirely hers."

Dr Luiz's gaze narrowed. "She mentioned she met you in Miami, but suggested it was a brief meeting. You sound as if you got to know her better than on a casual basis."

Matthew's comment to Natalie on the plane about knowing her popped into his head and his jaw tightened. "The entire conference was three days. I know very little about Dr. Sterling."

Just that she'd smiled lazily when he woke her up at sunrise so they could watch the sun come up that last morning. That she loved the feel of wet sand between her toes. That she laughed at the corny jokes he'd told her, and that she thought strawberries were manna from heaven.

That she made love to him like a siren and slept in his arms like an angel.

That she was going to be floored by the hospital's announcement today.

A knock sounded on Dr. Luiz's office door and Matthew tensed.

Natalie.

His heart pounded in his chest, thumping wildly against his ribcage.

He was about to play a role in hurting a woman who got to him as no other ever had.

Being in Memphis was right for Carrie.

That was what mattered most.

Natalie was just…just someone he'd once spent three fantasy days with.

CHAPTER SIX

WAITING FOR DR. LUIZ to bid her to enter his office, Natalie smoothed her scrubs.

Finally, she thought.

The buzz around the hospital was that something big was about to happen. Natalie knew what that something was. She couldn't wait until the announcement was made that she'd be promoted and that they'd gotten approval for the surgical procedure they'd been working on for years. She would soon perform the first in-utero vessel transposition repair at Memphis Children's.

A dream come true. She and Dr. Luiz's research showed great promise on correcting transposition of the vessels prior to birth. She'd gone through the procedure time and again on computer models, on premature and full-term "blue" babies. She wanted those babies to be born pink, to go home with their families much sooner, to have longer, healthier lives, and believed there was no reason they couldn't. That she would get to head up the team, would get to be lead surgeon, was enough to make a girl over the moon.

"Come in."

Smiling, Natalie turned the knob and stepped into Dr. Luiz's office, only to stop short when she realized her mentor wasn't alone.

She'd recognize the back of that dark head, those shoulders, anywhere.

What was Matthew doing in Dr. Luiz's office?

All the blood in her body drained to her feet, bolting them to the floor.

He had known it was her at the door. That much was evident when he stood and turned to meet her gaze. There was no surprise in his pale blue eyes.

Natalie fought shock, though, a million emotions hitting her at once.

He looked so good, so perfect, so much better than anything her memory could conjure. Her body leapt with joy, recalling how he'd stroked such pleasure through every part of her being.

But he shouldn't be there. At her work. With her boss.

Why was he there? What possible reason

could Matthew have for sitting in her boss's office?

Her brain raced. Had he told Dr. Luiz what had happened in Florida? Why would he? What did it matter if he had? The hospital had no say in whom she slept with. She doubted any of the board members cared, so long as she brought no public shame on the hospital.

Sex with Matthew was nothing any woman should be ashamed of. The man was gorgeous, brilliant, and had the ability to rock a woman's whole existence.

And how.

Nope, she was not going to let her brain go down that path.

Her gaze not wavering from his, Natalie resisted the urge to clear her throat. She would not let him know how much his being there threw her world off its axis.

"Natalie," Dr. Luiz began, "you'll, no doubt, recall having met Dr. Matthew Coleman in Miami, and I know you're a fan of his work."

Ha. She was a fan, but she doubted she and Dr. Luiz referred to the same work.

"Dr. Coleman." She reluctantly stuck out her hand. Reluctantly, because as much as she wanted to touch Matthew, for him to touch her, seeing him was wreaking havoc on her ability to think. "Nice to see you again."

Matthew's eyes searched hers, as if he was trying to determine if she believed her own words.

It *was* nice to see him. It was also making her heart pound like crazy, because he shouldn't be there. He should be a pleasant memory from her past. Nothing more.

Okay, so she hadn't been able to stop thinking about him, wanting him, but with time she would have shoved him into the recesses of her mind. At least, that had been the plan.

"Dr. Sterling," he greeted, taking her hand into his in what appeared to be a casual grasp yet was anything but. The skin-to-skin contact sent shockwaves throughout her body as surely as if he'd electrocuted her. How could he do that with just a brush of his skin against hers? "It's a pleasure to see you again."

Her cheeks heated. Mainly because Dr Luiz was observing their exchange. She tore her gaze from Matthew's and glanced at her very astute boss. Her boss who wouldn't quite meet her gaze.

Which had Natalie tugging her hand out of Matthew's scalding one.

In all the years Natalie had known Dr. Luiz, that was a first. He was the most straightforward person she'd ever met. So why was her boss avoiding making direct eye contact? She didn't understand Matthew's guilty look, and she sure didn't understand her boss's unusual behavior.

Her gaze narrowed suspiciously as she refocused on Matthew. "To what do we owe your unexpected visit?"

"Not unexpected. I invited him," Dr. Luiz informed, motioning to the vacant chair next to Matthew's. "Have a seat, Natalie."

Tension twisting in her muscles, tighter and tighter, Natalie sat.

"As you know, with my semi-retirement and the grant approval, there are a lot of upcoming changes taking place in our cardiology department."

Natalie's heart picked up pace, thundering in her chest.

"You and I have discussed that the hospital's main goal is to transform our department into one of the top facilities in the country, that we want to lead the way, rather than jumping on board with what other hospitals are doing."

This was one of those defining life moments.

Dreams were about to come true.

Only, why had he asked Matthew to be there? The only possible explanation, as crazy as it was, had her wondering if the dream was actually a nightmare.

"I'm pleased to inform you Dr. Coleman has joined our team to help us do just that, by taking my place as Head of Cardiology."

On a wave of extreme excitement and expected elation, Natalie's heart crashed down with the force of having been hit with a sledgehammer.

Nightmare it was.

Her blood drained from her face, heavily pooling in her legs, making her body feel stuck to her chair, making gravity suck at her entire being, threatening to flatten her.

Dr. Luiz was still talking but Natalie's ears roared, only letting her brain absorb part of what he was saying.

"...know you wanted the position..." *blah, blah, blah* "...know you are as ecstatic as I am about getting to work with Dr. Coleman..."

She should be, right? She'd admired Matthew's surgical work from afar for years. But she knew this department inside out, knew how to take it to the next level, and had earned the position.

Matthew had taken it from her.

"You'll be on his team, of course."

Of course. Her head spun.

"His second-in-command, with specific responsibilities…"

Second. Not in charge, but answering to Matthew.

Matthew. Oh, crap! Matthew was going to be in Memphis. All the time. Her eyes widened. Matthew was going to be working in Memphis. With her. Day after day.

Why?

Why would he do this?

Matthew watched emotions play across Natalie's face. None of them were good ones. She looked stunned, betrayed.

He hadn't betrayed her. He'd gone after the position before he'd met her. He needed the relocation. Carrie needed to be with people who could take care of her.

Despite Dr. Luiz's assurances that Natalie would be on board with the unexpected change, Matthew had known better. Then again, he knew the whole story, knew about their week-end fling.

Weekend fling. The label repulsed him, but it was what they'd shared.

Why the label bothered him so, he couldn't quite define. He'd had flings before. Several of them. None had left him feeling raw. Then again, he'd never been in quite this situation, either.

Regardless, he had a little girl to think of.

Carrie's counselor had advised Matthew to be sure to nurture the child over the next few months as she adapted to her new environment.

Nurture her. How did one do that exactly?

"As head of the surgery team, you'll be working closely with Matthew, of course."

Natalie's golden eyes blinked. "*I'm* heading up surgery? Not Dr. Coleman?"

That she asked something Dr. Luiz had just explained in detail attested to how in shock she was.

"As head of the entire department, Dr. Coleman will oversee your work, of course, but I can think of no one better for him to have on his leadership team than a heart surgeon of your caliber." Dr. Luiz pushed his gold-rimmed glasses up the bridge of his nose. "You knew I planned to step down, Natalie, and that I was counting on you to take on further responsibilities. Surely, this doesn't come as a surprise?"

"I'm surprised," Natalie immediately assured, face flushed. "Rather blown away. I thought..."

Everyone in the room knew what she'd thought.

"Never mind," she murmured, seeming to pull herself together. She turned toward Matthew, stuck out her hand again. "Congratulations, Dr. Coleman."

Matthew barely clasped her hand when she pulled it away, stood, and faced her former boss. "If there's nothing else?"

Dr. Luiz regarded her through narrowed lids, then shook his head.

Before Matthew could speak, Natalie was out the door and Dr. Luiz was talking again, but this time it was Matthew not registering what he was saying.

"Excuse me," he interrupted, not waiting for an answer as he took off after Natalie.

"Don't touch me," Natalie hissed when Matthew grabbed hold of her upper arm. Didn't he know she'd left the room in a hurry to escape him, to be alone, not to have him follow her?

Of course he did, but it hadn't mattered.

"That's not what you were saying a few weeks ago."

Suffering major shock for the second time that day, she spun and practically hissed at him, "How dare you say that?"

"Because it's true." His voice was calm, and that irritated her all the more.

He didn't have to point that particular truth out, she thought, glaring with all her might, hoping that her evil thoughts about him were readily seen on her face.

"But inappropriate for our current situation, don't you think?" she accused. He grimaced and she further attacked, "I don't want you here."

"I didn't think you did."

Flustered and just wanting to escape to her office to regroup her thoughts without him there to witness, she asked, "Then why are you here?"

He took a long breath. "That, my dearest Natalie, is a long story."

"I'm not your dearest Natalie. I'm not your anything."

Matthew raked his fingers through his inky hair, then glanced down the busy hospital corridor. "Is there somewhere we can go to talk?"

"Are you asking as my new boss?" Okay, her tone had been a bit snarky, but at the moment she didn't care. "Because otherwise, my answer is that we have nothing to say to each other. Not ever."

"Natalie—"

"Don't Natalie me. From the moment we said goodbye at the airport, I've been Dr. Sterling to you. Nothing more. Your three days expired long ago."

His expression taking on the dark and dangerous one he'd worn so well at the airport and on the plane, he nodded, as if her response didn't surprise him. Then again, why should he be surprised? He'd known what he was doing: stealing her dream job.

"Fine. As your new boss, is there somewhere we can talk in private?"

Without a word, Natalie led him down the corridor of offices. When she came to the one with her name on the brass plate, she punched in a code, then twisted the handle.

Opening the door, she paused, facing him. "I'm only letting you in because you're my boss now. No other reason."

His expression just as terse as her insides felt, he nodded. "Understood."

She moved aside, let him into her office, then shut the door behind her, wondering if she could claim temporary insanity if she lashed out at him for invading and upsetting her well-planned life.

If Matthew had had the slightest doubt as to Natalie's intentions on inviting him into her office, she'd made it clear before letting him pass through her doorway, and immediately began reiterating her feelings the moment the door clicked closed.

"Is this some kind of sick joke to you?"

"A joke?"

"Taking a job in Memphis." As if she couldn't be still, she paced across the room. "Why in the world would you leave your research in Boston?"

"I didn't leave my research, just relocated the parts I'll remain involved with to Memphis," he explained, wishing she'd sit down and let him tell her about the events that had led him to this moment.

Interest piqued, she lifted her brows. "Your research with the Libertine robot? How can you do that?"

"The Libertine research will continue in Boston, but it has gotten approval for use and will soon be available to other areas. Expanding my work to a second location, bringing my experience, will be of benefit to the medical community as a whole."

"You just happened to choose Memphis for this expansion?" She shook her head. "I'm not buying it."

"Even if I didn't have personal reasons, with Memphis Children's Hospital and St Jude's located here, it's a great location for my research. You can't deny that."

"Personal reasons?" She glared at him with pure loathing. "If you think for one minute your being here changes anything between us, you're wrong."

His being here changed everything, including how he could think of Natalie. What had been a pleasant interlude from reality had turned into a nightmare for them both.

"I chose Memphis before I ever met you."

As what he said sank in, her eyes widened. "You knew about this when we were in Miami? That you were moving to Memphis?"

Matthew raked his fingers through his hair again and sought for the right place to begin, to make her understand how they'd ended up in this exact moment.

"How *could* you?" she accused before he got a word out. "How could you smile and laugh

with me when you knew that we were going to
have to see each other day after day, that you
were going to be my boss. You had sex with
me anyway?"

The vehemence in her voice had him inter-
nally flinching, but he stood his ground. "When
I boarded that plane to Miami, I was under the
impression my moving to Memphis was a no-go
and Dr. Luiz's position would be filled by someone other than me."

"Right." She rolled her eyes. "You, the great
Dr. Matthew Coleman, interviewed for my job
and you thought they weren't going to hire you?
Puh-*lease*."

"I was never told it was your job, Natalie."
He wanted to be clear on that. "Dr. Luiz, nor
the board, ever mentioned any intent to offer
the position to you. Not once." She acted as if
he'd intentionally taken something of hers. He
hadn't done anything wrong. He'd needed this
opportunity in Memphis and when it was offered he'd taken it. "Were you told they were
going to offer you the position?"

The pain that flittered across her face stabbed
into Matthew's chest. Never had he wanted to
hurt Natalie. Far, far from it. But they needed
to clear the record on what had happened, to es-

tablish some professional ground rules if they were to work together. Maybe it would even be easier on them both if she hated him.

"No, but I was given reason to believe it would happen." Her face full of accusation, she asked, "For the record, if you had been aware of the possibility that the job would otherwise be mine, would it have changed anything?"

Technically, he *had* known it was a possibility, but even if he'd been point-blank told the job was hers if he said no, his reasons for wanting to relocate to Memphis took precedence.

Carrie took precedence.

He shook his head. "No."

A steely resolve settled into her eyes. "I don't want you here."

"I think you've already established that." He moved toward her, stopped when she flinched and backed away as if she couldn't stand the thought of him being close enough to touch her.

He rammed his hands into his pockets to keep from doing something stupid. Like doing just that. The last thing he needed was to touch Natalie. They were work colleagues now. Nothing more.

"My reasons for relocating have nothing to do with you," he assured. "I met with the hospital board and Dr. Luiz the day prior to flying to Miami, but the hospital initially wasn't willing to meet my terms. I thought that was the end of it, until Dr. Luiz called to say the board had reconsidered."

She didn't look any less ticked, just more suspicious. "When was that?"

"A month ago."

A fresh wave of betrayal blanched her already pale face. "Dr. Luiz has known for a month that the job was yours? He...he never said anything." She winced, paced back across the room, turned and met Matthew's gaze with a world of hurt shining in her eyes.

A desire to take away her hurt hit him, to somehow undo what had been done. Impossible. He knew that. But he hated his indirect role in the pain she was suffering.

"He should have told me. I deserved to know before an announcement was made."

"He told you today. Before an announcement was made," Matthew pointed out. "He has great respect for you. He was adamant you have a prestigious place on my team."

"As your second-in-command," she bit out, not impressed. "Just as I'm *his* second-in-command."

"You're young, Natalie."

"What does that have to do with anything?" she huffed. "I have been with Dr. Luiz for years. Did my residency at Memphis Children's. I've worked my butt off to build our neonatal cardiology program. I'm more than qualified. What does my age have to do with anything?"

She was right. Had Matthew not intervened, she would have been named Head of Neonatal Cardiology with Dr. Luiz's semi-retirement.

"I don't know what to tell you, Natalie. I can't speak for Dr. Luiz or the hospital board. I interviewed for a position that I needed, and when my terms were met, I accepted."

"That you needed?" she scoffed. "You head up your team in Boston at one of the most prestigious hospitals in the world. Why come here?"

She was right. He'd never have chosen to leave Boston had it been just him involved.

"Relocating to Memphis makes Carrie's life better."

Taken aback, she stared at him, then asked in a voice he barely recognized, "Who is Carrie?"

Matthew took a deep breath. "My…daughter."

CHAPTER SEVEN

THE HOSPITAL WAS abuzz with news of the handsome new heart surgeon taking Dr. Luiz's place. How wonderful for the hospital that such a gifted surgeon had taken over their department. *Blah, blah, blah.* Natalie was sick of hearing about Matthew.

Sick. Of. It.

She simply could not escape him.

At work, everyone was talking about him.

At home, he invaded her sleep.

With her friends, well, she was seriously considering placing ads for their replacements if they didn't quit going on about how lucky she was that her fabulous holiday lover had shown back up in her life. Permanently.

"You're thinking hard on something," Dr. Luiz said, drawing Natalie's attention to where he had entered the break room just off the neonatal cardiac care unit where Natalie had made rounds. She'd stopped to get a cup of coffee because she'd been dragging.

She'd been dragging since she walked into Dr. Luiz's office expecting to celebrate the culmination of years of hard work and instead had come face to face with her vacation fling.

Stirring the one packet of sugar she'd added to her cup with a tiny red straw, Natalie cut her gaze to Dr. Luiz, but didn't meet his eyes. How could she, when she felt so betrayed?

"It's been a busy morning," she mumbled.

She'd had two new patient consults, plus had checked in on a five-day-old who she hoped to be able to transfer to a step-down unit soon.

Besides, what else could she say? She couldn't really scream and yell at Dr. Luiz, could she? If so, what would she say? That she felt as if a man she'd trusted, her mentor, had betrayed her by bringing in Matthew?

"The Harris case?" She *should* have been thinking about the Harris case rather than what, or more truthfully, who, she couldn't get off her brain. "The board approved the procedure," Dr. Luiz continued. "I thought you'd have scheduled the surgery the moment the board gave you a thumbs-up."

"I'm not sure Delaine Harris is the right first case."

She'd been over and over the woman's file. Delaine Harris was twenty-five years old and was pregnant with her first child. She'd already signed consent forms for the experimental procedure. They'd only been waiting on the board's approval, which had come through the day before. At just under five months pregnant, Delaine had known her baby's heart didn't work properly due to her vessels being transposed since her first ultrasound. If they were going to do the surgery in utero, precious time was ticking away.

Timing was everything.

Natalie wanted to make sure Delaine Harris's baby had every fighting chance and that doing the procedure in utero improved those odds, that nothing went wrong.

"Any particular reason why?"

None that she wanted to share.

Which was disconcerting, as she'd always discussed everything with Dr. Luiz. He'd mentored her from day one of her residency, when she'd been lucky enough to work with him.

Now, because of the situation with Matthew, she felt as if he'd let her down. Logically, she knew that wasn't what had happened, but it wasn't logic guiding her emotions.

"I've known you too long not to recognize that you're upset about Dr. Coleman."

Yeah, he'd also known her long enough to know she'd expected to be in Matthew's place. Still, what could she say? Dr. Luiz and the board had done what they believed was best for the hospital. She couldn't present a valid argument that said otherwise.

"He's an excellent pediatric heart surgeon," she said, for the sole reason that Dr. Luiz waited for a response.

"He's someone whose work you've admired for years."

"True." But only because he hadn't snatched her dream job. Which was unfair, but she didn't care. Fair quit being a priority when he'd slept with her knowing he'd interviewed for her job and he hadn't bothered telling her.

"It caught the board and myself off guard when he approached us about working at Memphis Children's."

"I can imagine." For all her gruff over Matthew being at her hospital, she did recognize his credentials.

"He's told you his reasons?"

Oh, he'd told her all right. He had a daughter.

She'd not let him tell her more. She hadn't wanted to know, because at this point, what had it mattered?

A daughter.

That seemed like a big something to have not mentioned while they'd been in Miami.

While they'd been in bed and...

She took a sip of her coffee, ignoring that the hot liquid scalded her tongue.

He hadn't lied to her. Not exactly. He'd said he wasn't married or involved with anyone, but he hadn't said he didn't have children. Not that she'd asked. Silly her. She'd add that to her list of things to know about a man before sleeping with him.

Ha. As if. Between Jonathan and Matthew, she was finished with men.

Not that she supposed Matthew's being a father mattered for their weekend purposes. Still, a woman should know something like that about a man she spent three days having sex with.

She should also know if he was vying for her job.

"I never met Dr. Fisk, but I think it's admirable what Matthew is doing to raise that little girl."

Dr. Fisk. So, the girl's mother had been a doctor. Why was Matthew raising the child on his own? Had something happened to "Dr. Fisk" or had the woman walked away?

The question of the girl's mother had haunted Natalie for the past week, but she'd refused to talk to him further about it. She just wanted to forget Miami, to forget him.

Pain throbbed at her temple and she resisted the urge to massage the ache.

What did it matter why he was raising the girl by himself? It was nothing to do with Natalie. He was nothing to her.

Other than that he had ousted her from her dream job and she'd once spent a weekend all wrapped up in him. No big deal.

Despite the fact she'd barely touched her coffee, she poured the remainder down the sink. "If you'll excuse me, I need to get back to clinic. I've a full day ahead."

Dr. Luiz nodded, but not before giving her a knowing look.

What he thought he knew, Natalie wasn't sure, but she made her escape before he asked about things she didn't want to think about, much less discuss.

In a private examination room off the Neonatal Intensive Cardiac Care Unit, Natalie ran the ultrasound wand over the tiny chest of Andrea Smith, studying the monitor as she did so.

"Shh, it's okay," the baby's mother cooed, holding the six-pound baby in her arms. "Is her heart any better?"

Wishing she could offer the new mother affirmation, Natalie continued to run the wand over the baby's chest and told her, "I'll go over the results when I've finished having a look."

The mother winced. "Sorry. I'm just so anxious to know how she is."

Natalie glanced away from the monitor long enough to offer the woman an empathetic smile. "It's okay. I understand. It's just better if I finish the test, so I can give you a more complete answer."

When done, Natalie didn't have good news. The child would have to have surgery sooner rather than later to repair the aortic arch hypoplasia and left ventricle size deformities the child had been born with. She called the operating room scheduler and set the wheels in motion to take the child to surgery for repair.

Imagine her surprise the following morning when, after scrubbing in, she joined the rest of her surgery team and had an unexpected member with the palest blue eyes she'd ever looked into.

"What are you doing here?" she asked, unable to stop herself. *Be professional, Natalie.* In front of the surgical crew wasn't the place to air her animosity.

"Scrubbing in as second."

"Shouldn't you have given me a heads-up you'd be taking Dr. Bingham's place?"

"No better way to learn how things work at Memphis Children's than to jump right in."

More than two hours later, while struggling to get the aortic valve leaflets to precisely lie as they should, Natalie became more and more frustrated that she was under Matthew's watchful eye, blaming him rather than the difficult nature of the surgery.

"May I?" he asked at one point, causing Natalie's gaze to lift to his astute one.

Seriously? What was she supposed to say? Although Dr. Luiz's official partial retirement date hadn't yet arrived, Matthew was her boss.

She watched with reluctant fascination as he made a deeper cut in a modified Ross procedure and then meticulously worked to repair the uncooperative valve leaflets.

When he was done, the flaps fell into place perfectly between each beat.

Ecstatic for her patient and what should be a great surgical outcome, Natalie found her annoyance with Matthew slipping a little over her excitement at what she'd just witnessed.

How could she be annoyed with him when what he'd just done had been nothing short of genius?

If only she hadn't had sex with him.

When their tiny two-day-old patient was off to Recovery, Natalie was all too aware of Matthew beside her as she left the operating room and slipped off her protective gear.

"Tell me why that worked so well, what it's called, and if it's something you've been working on for a while or just came up with."

Stripping off his protective gear, Matthew regarded her. "You know the Ross procedure?"

"What you did was a modified version. I caught that. When you were finished, the valve leaflets fell perfectly."

"Only because you did a great job with the resection on the ventricle," he praised, leaning against a long sink used for scrubbing. "Otherwise, what I did wouldn't have worked."

"You've done this before, then?"

"A few times."

"Success rate?"

"So far we're at one hundred percent."

Natalie's eyes widened. "Seriously? What are the parameters?"

"I did my first one just over a year ago. About a year and a half ago, now," he amended. "Currently, she's had no further need of surgery."

"Valve is growing with the body? No issues with scar tissue causing stenosis?"

"Thus far, it's a success, but we won't know for sure until Kenzie gets older."

Kenzie. The name clicked.

"I read about her," Natalie admitted, wishing his work didn't fascinate her so much, wishing there wasn't a hint of a smile in his eyes. "You used the Libertine robot during that procedure."

"Yes."

"She had other heart issues." She thought back. "Something to do with her pulmonic valve."

He seemed surprised. "That's right. I did a repair of her pulmonic and aortic valves."

"I read the piece you published on the procedure, but I don't recall anything about what you just did on my patient."

"There wasn't anything in the article about

what I just did. The article was about the Libertine, not the specifics of the valve repair. I've done that particular procedure a total of five times, including the one I just did. More research needs to be done prior to anything being published."

"Did you record Kenzie's surgery?"

His lips curved into a smile. "You want to watch my private stash?"

Natalie did.

But she didn't.

But she really, really did. If she was going to have to put up with him being in Memphis, being at her hospital, she should have some perks, right?

"Would you let me?"

He didn't hesitate, just held her gaze. "I would."

"Because you want to further the knowledge of your staff?" Why she pushed, she wouldn't delve deeply to label, just that she wanted his clarification.

"Because you asked," he corrected, his gaze locked with hers. "Although, you're right. Part of my position is to further my staff's knowledge. The hospital is great, otherwise I wouldn't have considered the move. But I hope to bring positive changes. Dr. Luiz suggested I discuss those with you as he thought some of our ideas overlapped, and you could be key in the implementation process."

He was completely sincere, and Natalie found herself being sucked into the idea of working with someone who'd been operating on the cutting edge his entire career. He'd been at a hospital with the resources to make history, not follow in its footsteps. He wanted to bring that to her hospital.

"If we hadn't met in Miami and you hadn't stolen my dream job, I might like working with you," she admitted, somewhat reluctantly.

He studied her a moment, then asked, "Do you expect me to say I'm sorry, Natalie? I won't." He had that dark and dangerous look about him that had her glancing away. "I'm not."

For Miami or taking her dream job? *Or both?* Natalie wondered. Either way, her adrenaline rush from the successful procedure and watching his innovative surgical technique was wearing her down, leaving her restless and needing to get away.

"Are you going to the retirement party for Dr. Luiz?" he asked.

The party was almost two weeks away, sponsored by the hospital, and a big deal.

"What kind of question is that?" The man had been her mentor since residency. "Of course I'm going. Just because he sold me out to the board in favor of you doesn't mean I'd bail on his retirement party."

Matthew's expression tightened. "Is that really how you see what he did?"

Natalie closed her eyes, took a deep breath. "He did what was right for the cardiology department, for the hospital, and for Memphis. I don't fault him for that."

"Sure you do."

He was right. She did.

"I understand why he did what he did." She did understand why the board preferred Matthew. "What I don't understand is why you left an amazing hospital and research facility to come here."

A weary look crossed his face so briefly that Natalie wasn't sure she hadn't imagined it. Maybe she had, because he just shrugged and said, "I like a challenge."

"Ha. Getting this hospital anywhere close to what you left is going to be a challenge. An impossible one, because we don't have the funding you're used to."

He studied her a moment, then shrugged again. "Sometimes challenges can be a good thing."

"You should bring a date," Monica encouraged as Suzie nodded her agreement, and Natalie wished her friends would find a new topic of conversation.

Every time she saw them all they wanted to discuss was Matthew. When was the last time she saw him? What did he say? What did he do? It was getting old.

"Make him jealous."

Natalie rolled her eyes. "I don't want to make him jealous. I want…"

She wasn't sure what she wanted. Honestly, she understood the hospital hiring Matthew. He was brilliant. The man had been improving pediatric cardiac outcomes for over a decade and the entire hospital was ecstatic to have him join them.

If only Natalie could feel that same joy.

On a personal level, she knew it would have been better never to see him again.

On a professional level, he'd taken the job she wanted.

She resented that he'd invaded her life and turned everything topsy-turvy. Yet she couldn't stop thinking about him, even now as she gave all she had to the elliptical machine. Monica was to her right, Suzie to the left. All three of them had worked up a sweat.

"What is it you want, Natalie?" Suzie insisted when Natalie didn't finish her comment.

To forget Miami and her career goals so she could join the ranks of her coworkers, ecstatic that someone of Matthew's caliber had joined their team.

Wasn't going to happen, but it would help if she could.

Looking at him did wacky things to her insides. Like throw her heart rhythm and make her lungs forget how to diffuse oxygen. As much as she'd like to blame Miami, how her body reacted to Matthew was instinctive rather than a Pavlovian response.

Although memories of Matthew's kisses, his touch, his... *No, no, no.* She sped up the movement of her legs as fast she could go, faster, faster, faster. *Forget Miami.*

Obviously he had. Not once had he made one

untoward move around her. Other than their first few encounters at the hospital, he'd been professional and, if anything, a bit aloof, as if he didn't want there to be any misunderstandings of his intentions.

"In case you've forgotten," she huffed out as she struggled to maintain her crazy pace, "I haven't been on a date since Jonathan and I broke things off. Not counting Miami—and Miami doesn't count."

"Speaking of the ex, did you hear that the bimbo he was messing around with is wearing an engagement ring?"

Monica's question curled Natalie's nose. "Better her than me. I don't want the man or the ring."

Monica smiled. "I'm so glad you're over him."

Sadly, she was over him before it was over. She'd cared about him, but she'd never needed him. Or craved him. Or thought about him all the time.

"What are you going to do about Matthew?"

Ignoring the sweat running down her brow, Natalie kept moving, pushing harder and harder against the elliptical. "Absolutely nothing. He was supposed to be just a pleasant memory, but I didn't get that lucky."

"Some would say him showing back up in your life makes you lucky," Suzie pointed out.

"Yeah, well, I'm not a girl who wants to be face to face with a man she thought she was only spending a weekend with."

"Maybe you need to rethink that."

"Rethink what?"

"Just spending that one weekend with him. Monica and I are going to dress you up for Friday night's party and you should go for it."

"For old times' sake," Suzie added.

"Uh-uh. Getting involved with Matthew, my boss, is the last thing I need to do."

"Why?"

"Shall I count the reasons?" At her friends' expectant looks, Natalie continued. "One, he took my dream job." Her friends didn't seem impressed at the gravity of just how devastated she was. "Two, he's my boss." Again, her friends didn't seem to understand what that implied. "Three, he has a kid."

"I'm not seeing a problem," Suzie said.

"The last thing I'd want is to get involved with a man who has kids."

"What's the deal with this kid, anyway? He never mentioned her in Miami?"

"No, and I don't know."

"You should ask him."

"Why would I do that?"

"Because you want to know."

"You mean *you* want to know," Natalie corrected, cycling as fast as she could on the elliptical.

"Protest all you want, Natalie, but this guy gets to you."

"Not in a good way."

Both her friends had the audacity to laugh.

CHAPTER EIGHT

NATALIE STARED AT the quiet little girl playing on a tablet computer in Matthew's office.

His daughter? Had to be.

Natalie wanted to turn and run, because she didn't want to be confronted with the child. She wasn't sure of all the reasons why, just that a self-defensive part of her warned to run. But the girl looked up from her game and met Natalie's gaze with big brown eyes, stopping any unnoticed retreat.

Although she was beautiful, Natalie couldn't help but think it was a shame the girl hadn't inherited Matthew's unusual pale blue eye color or his dark features. Still, with her sagging ponytail, dimpled cheeks and big eyes, the girl was undeniably adorable.

"Hi! Uncle Matthew isn't here."

Uncle Matthew? Why had the girl called him "Uncle", and what was Matthew doing leaving the girl unattended in his office? Natalie knew next to nothing about parenting, but she knew enough to know that one didn't leave a small child by herself.

"He's in an important meeting. Stephanie," the name came out with a cute hesitation of each syllable as the girl made sure she said the name correctly, "is watching me."

Only Stephanie was nowhere to be seen.

"Where is Stephanie?"

"The bathroom. She wasn't feeling good and keeps going to the bathroom." The child wrinkled her nose. "She has diarrhea." Again, she put emphasis on each syllable to make sure she properly enunciated.

"Poor Stephanie," Natalie commiserated, not sure whether to walk away or to stay. The kid was too young to be by herself. "I'm Natalie. What's your name?"

Why did this conversation feel so weird? She was a pediatric heart surgeon. She dealt with children on an almost daily basis. Why were her palms clammy?

"Carrie. I'm four. Do you want to see my game?"

No, Natalie didn't. She wanted far, far away from the evidence of Matthew's deceit—but the hopeful look on the child's face left her unable to do anything more than cross to where the little girl sat. She stooped down.

"What kind of game is it?"

"A fashion game." Carrie's eyes lit up as if it was the most fabulous game ever. "See all the pretty clothes?"

Natalie had never been a girly girl and fashion wasn't her forte, but she nodded her agreement as she studied each item the child clicked on.

Big brown eyes regarded her. "Which one is your favorite?"

"They're all great," she assured, studying the colored images. "Which makes it difficult to choose, but I like the blue dress best."

She nodded as if she'd expected Natalie to say as much. "That's Uncle Matthew's favorite, too. It's the color of his eyes and makes me think of a robin's egg."

There went the "Uncle Matthew" again. And there went Natalie's cheeks, bursting into flames. "That's not why I liked it best."

"It's the mermaid tail, isn't it?" Carrie said with a knowing tone.

"The what?"

The little girl pointed at the screen. "The skirt. It's why you like that dress? My mommy's wedding dress had a mermaid tail. It's my favorite, too. I like clothes, especially mermaid tails."

Her mommy's wedding dress. Matthew had been married to the girl's mother once upon a time. Where was she now?

"Um, yes. The mermaid tail." Thinking her conversation with the child was getting more and more awkward, she stared at the computer screen. What she really wanted to do was get out of Dodge, but she couldn't bring herself to leave the girl alone, so she resolved to stick around until Stephanie got back from the bathroom. Still, a subject change was overdue. "How does your game work? You design the clothes and then fill in the colors?"

Carrie happily demonstrated how to select and manipulate an item on the screen with a stylus pen. "You want to try?"

"I'd rather watch you. I'm not much on clothes or fashion."

The girl studied her scrubs then nodded. "I can tell. Pretty boring."

In spite of how awkward she felt, Natalie laughed. "We should send a memo to my new boss to up the appeal of our hospital wardrobe, eh? Maybe add some mermaid tail scrubs."

Natalie's boss thought her appeal was just fine

as was. More than fine. Of course, Matthew wasn't thinking of her hospital wardrobe, just the woman. Not that he should be allowing himself to think of her as anything except a fellow neonatal heart surgeon and colleague.

Why did he keep struggling with that? Of course, he knew. Miami. How was he supposed to relegate her to a mere coworker when he knew just how hot her fire burned?

When he'd finished with his meeting and returned to his office to collect Carrie, he'd expected to find the nursing assistant with her. Running the little girl to his mother's place on his day off for the hour or less the meeting would take seemed unnecessary, but yet again it seemed he'd made a bad parenting judgment call, because Stephanie was nowhere to be seen.

Still, finding Natalie stooped next to Carrie was a pleasant surprise, especially since much of the meeting he'd just attended had involved Natalie and her role in the department.

"Oh, Dr Coleman!" Stephanie gushed, hastening behind him. "Glad you're back."

"Speaking of being back…" he frowned at the nursing assistant he'd thought he could trust "…where have you been?"

The woman's face reddened. "Sorry, sir, but

I've developed an awful case of what I think is food poisoning. Now that you're back, I'm checking in with my nurse manager, clocking out and heading home to the privacy of my own bathroom."

"She has diarrhea," Carrie piped up from where she sat at his desk, making the word four syllables.

The nursing assistant's flush brightened even more.

"Yeah, well, glad you're back," the young woman said, then to Carrie, "Maybe next time we meet I won't get sick. Dr. Sterling," she acknowledged Natalie, then disappeared.

"Thank you for staying with Carrie while Stephanie was otherwise occupied."

Looking uncomfortable, Natalie stood, smoothing her hands over her scrubs. "She was showing me her designs."

"Carrie plans to take the fashion world by storm someday, don't you, kiddo?"

Rather than answer his question, Carrie lifted big eyes to him and reminded him of something else he should have done prior to the meeting, but had run out of time when she'd not cooperated in his trying to get her dressed.

"Can we go eat now?"

Had he fed her breakfast? He thought so…

"Soon," he told her guiltily, wondering if he had a protein bar in his desk he could give her to tide her over for another thirty minutes or so. "I need to finish a few things here, then we'll go." Was it wrong of him to make her wait while he finished? He couldn't see leaving to eat and then having to drag her back by the hospital afterwards.

"Can Natalie go with us?"

Matthew watched Natalie's expression tighten and started to come up with a reason why that wasn't a good idea, because the last thing he needed was to spend time with her outside the hospital. But the color draining from her face and an onslaught of frustrated pride had him saying, "Of course she can go with us."

Natalie's eyes widened and she gave him a warning look. "Sorry, I've a dozen things to do before I leave for dinner."

"We could wait on you," Carrie offered, looking way too eager for Natalie to say yes, especially as Matthew knew she was hungry.

Natalie's cheeks flushed. "I'd hate for you to have to do that."

"We don't mind, do we?" Carrie looked up at him expectantly, making him feel a jerk for having let her think there was any hope of Natalie going with them. Why had he?

Because whether he wanted to or not, he *liked* the idea of Natalie going with them. She'd seemed comfortable with Carrie, as though she knew what she was doing while she'd been sitting next to her looking at her tablet.

"We want to make new friends, right?" the child continued. "I could show you more of my game. There are more dresses with mermaid tails!"

Natalie was looking downright panicked. Matthew toyed with the idea of letting her off the hook, but he was curious as to why Carrie was so eager for her to go with them. Other than with regard to his mother, sister and nieces, she'd not shown interest in making new friends or getting to know anyone. Until Natalie. Go figure.

"That's right," he agreed. "Plus, I owe you for sitting with my favorite fashionista."

"I was only here for, like, five minutes," Natalie rushed to clarify. "Ten at the most. You owe me nothing."

Her comment reminded him of her teasing in Miami. He'd liked owing Natalie because the paying up had been a lot of fun.

"Please?" Carrie pleaded in her most appealing voice, the one Matthew hadn't learned to say no to. "He'll take us to get really great food…" She named the restaurant they'd visited way too often over the past few weeks. Matthew didn't normally eat fast food, but apparently kids loved it.

Natalie's nose wrinkled and she frowned at him. "Not a very healthy choice for a four-year-old, is it?"

Probably not, but he'd just been so grateful when Carrie had started eating again that he'd fed her whatever she wanted. Still, as a cardiologist, he knew the dangers of too much high-fat, low-nutrition food and should have been making Carrie eat healthy. Another thing to feel guilty over.

Carrie turned pleading eyes toward Natalie. "Please say you'll go. *You* can pick the restaurant."

Still Natalie hesitated. If she could have thought of a way to get out of going, she would have. That was written all over her face.

Sensing Natalie was about to make a break for it, Carrie launched into a new plea. "I'll be extra-good and eat something healthy. I promise!"

"You're always extra-good." Matthew tugged on her lopsided ponytail, wondering how it had worked loose when he'd thought he'd finally gotten it right. Then again, she acted as if he were ripping her hair out every time he brushed it or went to pull it up. He wouldn't take back his comment, though. She'd dealt with so much that he figured a little acting out here and there was normal.

Carrie lifted her big eyes to Natalie again. "Please. Don't you want to be my friend?"

How had Natalie gotten manipulated into this? She still wasn't quite sure. The last two people on earth she wanted to be having dinner with were Matthew and his daughter.

She wasn't sure Matthew wanted her there any more than she wanted to be there.

Yet she sat at the organic food restaurant, eating kale chips and freshly made salsa one after another to give her hands something to do while observing Matthew with Carrie.

He obviously loved the girl. Which seemed an odd thing to think. Of course Matthew loved his daughter.

The girl obviously adored him as well.

But there was something about their relationship that didn't feel quite right, almost an awkwardness in how Matthew regarded her and how she regarded him. Still, Carrie truly had been well-behaved, had listened closely to her menu options but then let Natalie choose her meal for her, promising to eat every bite.

They'd been at the restaurant about fifteen minutes when the child dropped a bombshell that caused Natalie to almost choke on a chip.

"My mommy and daddy died in an airplane crash and I live with Uncle Matthew now." The child kept talking, very matter-of-fact, but Natalie didn't catch anything else she said.

Just that her mommy and daddy had died.

Which brought back some terrible memories of her own, and gave Natalie a whole new empathy for the girl. Eyes blurring, she took a drink of her water, wishing she'd ordered something a lot stiffer, then offered, "I'm sorry about your mom and dad. My parents died when I was young, too."

Why had she offered that last tidbit? Matthew didn't need to know about her sordid childhood. Nor did she need to form any connection with this child.

"Did they die in a plane crash?" Carrie asked

at the same time as Matthew's leg brushed up against her from across the table and he said,

"I'm sorry."

She didn't want his sympathy. She didn't want anything from him. Or Carrie. Just...

"No," she managed, hating that her eyes watered. "But they were in an accident. A car wreck." She fought the sadness that threatened her when she recalled the horror of losing her parents. "It was a long time ago. I was around your age."

"It feels like forever since my mommy and daddy died." Carrie turned sad eyes on Matthew. "How long has it been?"

"Just over four months."

Four months. That wasn't long ago. Poor Carrie. How had Matthew ended up with the girl?

"Carrie's parents were my best friends," he said, seeming to have read her mind. "I was her godfather and now she's stuck with me."

In the way that children do, Carrie jumped to another topic. "Did you know that a baby giraffe is about to be born at the zoo?"

Natalie shook her head.

"It's so exciting!" Carrie continued, her eyes glowing. "You can watch the momma giraffe online and they have a special app for your phone. Do you have it?"

Again, Natalie shook her head.

"You should get it so you know when Zoie is about to be born."

"Zoie?"

"That's what they're going to call the baby giraffe. It's a girl. The zoo held a contest on naming her and Zoie won. You want the app?"

"Um, maybe."

"I can help you," Carrie offered, reaching for Natalie's phone.

Not sure whether she should trust a four-year-old with her phone or whether she wanted a zoo app to notify her about a giraffe, Natalie handed the device to Carrie.

She tapped several buttons, explaining to Natalie each step of the way, as if Natalie were the child and Carrie the adult.

"There," she said, handing the phone back. "Now you have the zoo app and you'll get Zoie updates."

"Thank you," Natalie said, sliding the phone into her scrubs pocket.

"Uncle Matthew says I can have a puppy soon as we get settled."

"A puppy?" Natalie had never owned a pet.

Her foster parents had often said it was enough work raising her without adding an animal to the mix. A few of them had acted as if *Natalie* were an animal... To redirect her thoughts, she met Matthew's gaze. "Are you sure? I hear puppies are a lot of work."

"It's not as cool as a baby giraffe, and I'd rather have a big dog," Carrie interjected, "but Uncle Matthew says I have to pick a small one that can stay in the house because we're gone so much." Carrie wrinkled her nose. "But if we get a puppy we shouldn't be gone so much, especially if it's a little puppy."

Natalie lifted her gaze to Matthew.

"She makes sense, and," he bent to Carrie's level, "I'm working on being home more. That's why we're in Memphis, remember?"

"To be near Grandma and Aunt Elaine and Mandy and Liz. They are excited about the giraffe, too."

So much began to click.

"I guess it is easier living closer to your family," Natalie mused, then went hot-cheeked, straightened, and brushed her hands over her scrubs. "Not that it's any of my business."

"Oh, it is definitely better being close to my family. My mom's awesome. Since I couldn't convince her to move away from the rest of the family to come live with me in Boston, we came here."

Natalie traced her finger over the rim of her water glass. "Do you have a big family?"

"Big enough. A sister and several aunts, uncles and cousins. It's a few years since I've been to a family get-together, but they're unforgettable." He shook his head as if recalling past holidays. "They can get a little crazy."

Having little memory of any family other than what she could recall of her parents, Natalie struggled to imagine what it must be like at those holiday gatherings.

How many times over the years had she longed to belong to a family? To make memories like the ones Matthew was obviously recalling? How could he have missed family holiday gatherings? Didn't he realize how blessed he was?

She stuffed another kale chip in her mouth.

"Do you have kids I could play with, too, Natalie?"

Coughing to clear her throat of the chip that lodged there, Natalie shook her head. "No, I don't have any kids."

Carrie's brows veed together and she shook

her head, making her ponytail sag further. "Well, that's just sad."

Yes, Natalie supposed it was, but bringing a child into the world just so she wouldn't be alone would be just as sad. She'd once thought she'd meet someone who would want to stick around, who wouldn't leave her, who'd want to have babies with her. But after Jonathan's betrayal she wasn't so sure. Maybe some people weren't meant to ever be a part of a real family. Certainly she never had been.

"Some people might think so, but I'm not sad. My life is very full," she defended, not wanting the child or Matthew to feel sorry for her. At Carrie's continued look of skepticism, Natalie continued, "I'm quite happy with my life, really."

Mostly, she told the truth. Except for the part where Matthew had taken her job and occupied her thoughts.

"Here, let me fix your ponytail before your hair gets in your food," Natalie offered, removing the loose band and using her fingers to comb Carrie's hair back into a ponytail.

Natalie could feel Matthew's hot scrutiny and finally she looked up, meeting his eyes.

"You make that look easy."

Natalie shrugged. "Not much to it."

"Maybe not, since she sat perfectly still for you." Matthew gave Carrie a pointed look.

"She didn't hurt me," the child defended, then gave Natalie an exasperated look. "He pulls my hair out when he does it!"

"I'm getting better," Matthew assured, his expression almost one of need for Carrie to reassure him that he truly was improving. Carrie gave Natalie a look that said she didn't agree with Matthew's assessment, then rattled on in her four-year-old chatter about how her mother had used to style her hair.

Finding herself wanting to give Matthew that reassurance, Natalie stopped herself. She shouldn't be here, shouldn't be seeing this side of Matthew. A side where a renowned heart surgeon who topped his field took on raising an orphaned child who had no one else, even when it meant giving up a job he loved and becoming a fish-out-of-water parent.

She stared at him, fighting a barrage of swirling emotions.

Oh, good grief. The last thing she needed was to soften toward a man who was supposed to have only been a three-day vacation affair and had ended up turning her life topsy-turvy.

* * *

Natalie loved her patients. From the tiny babies to the teenagers she cared for, she never felt awkward or self-conscious. The only other children she'd been around had been other foster children. Kids who'd been down on their luck and as defensive as she was.

Then there'd been the birth children of the foster families. The loved children who'd often seen her as inferior and felt they had the right to lord it over her, to abuse her verbally and sometimes physically.

She hadn't gotten close to any of them, had more negative memories than positive ones about those encounters, and would forever be grateful for the final foster family who'd taken her in when she'd been fourteen. She'd stayed with the McCulloughs until she'd left for college. They'd never had children of their own, but had raised several foster kids. It was after she'd been taken in by that wonderful couple that she'd met Suzie and Monica and made her first real friends.

None of that had prepared her for Matthew's daughter and the bond she already felt with the orphaned little girl.

Dinner had been interesting. They'd eaten

their healthy dinner while Carrie told Natalie about going to the park with her grandmother the day before.

"I was only supposed to be at the hospital for less than an hour or she'd have gone to Grandma's today," Matthew added.

"Uncle Matthew used to take me to the hospital a lot before we moved." Carrie didn't sound happy about the memory.

"Now that we're closer to Grandma, that shouldn't happen too much. Plus, Aunt Elaine can watch you some and has a list of sitters for me to interview. You shouldn't get stuck going too often once I get settled in at work." Matthew turned to Natalie. "She doesn't like going to the hospital."

"Because you take so long," Carrie reminded.

"Because I take so long," he agreed, then tried to lighten the mood. "And because the hospital isn't the place for high fashion. She'd much rather I take her to the mall."

Natalie found herself wanting to defend Matthew, to help Carrie see how difficult it must have been for him to have had a child thrust into his busy life.

"You could use your hospital trips as research to design us new scrubs with the mermaid tail like we talked about earlier," Natalie suggested, trying to ease the underlying tension between Matthew and the child.

The girl's nose wrinkled. "Scrubs are boring clothes."

Natalie glanced down at the blue ones she wore. "Completely boring."

Yet they were her preferred wardrobe and what she had on more often than not.

"Which is why doctors and nurses around the world need you to come up with something stylish for us. Help us be more fashionable."

Carrie seemed intrigued by that idea, and she and Natalie carried on a quite lengthy conversation about hospital fashion.

The conversation jumped from one topic to another and before Natalie knew it she was at Matthew's house. How had that happened? She'd had no intention of going to his house. Or spending one second more with him and his daughter than was absolutely necessary.

Only Carrie had wanted to show off her new bedroom, something she was excited about and super-proud of. Natalie hadn't had the heart to say no, and when she'd looked at Matthew for guidance he'd just shrugged as if to say he didn't care one way or the other.

She supposed he didn't.

Since his Memphis arrival, he'd been professional and nothing more. He'd probably forgotten all about Miami. It was what she needed to do. What she wanted to do.

For most of dinner, he'd listened to her and Carrie's conversation, throwing in a comment here and there, but almost seeming as if he was studying their interactions.

His house was in an upscale neighborhood on Mud Island not too far from where she lived, and just ten minutes from the hospital. A modern brick monstrosity within a gated community with a circle drive and a fenced back yard. It was a house for a family, not two people.

"Excuse the lack of furniture. I sold most of what I had in Boston, rather than move it. Carrie and I are working on buying furniture as time allows. It's our weekend project to put our home together piece by piece."

"Let me show you my room!" Carrie grabbed Natalie's hand and led her through the mostly empty house.

When she pushed open a door, Natalie expected little more than a bare room with a bed, or perhaps a cot. Instead, it was as if she'd stepped into a fantasy.

The opposite wall from the door housed a painted wooden floor-to-ceiling castle with a stairwell leading up to a tower with only a small peek hole. The walls were painted in a fairyland motif, complete with another far, far away castle, unicorns and other friendly-looking animals, puffy white clouds, blue skies and rainbows, and even a waterfall.

"Wow," Natalie breathed, taking in the room. "Just wow."

"I know," Carrie agreed, sounding a bit breathless herself.

Natalie walked over to the bed, with its pink comforter and sheer white drapes that gave it a mystical tent appearance.

"Don't you just love it?" Carrie whispered, clasping her hands together.

"I want to move in here." She turned to Matthew. "You did this?"

"Carrie found photos of what she wanted. We picked out the key pieces of furniture and I hired a decorating firm to make it happen. My mother oversaw the work while Carrie and I were wrapping up in Boston."

"Is the decorator doing the rest of the house?"

"We may enlist her help again," he admitted,

"but for now I had her to do my room, Carrie's room and the kitchen."

"You have castles in your bedroom, too?"

He shook his head. "No castles or unicorns. Not even a princess."

"You have me," Carrie reminded. "I'm a princess."

"That I do," Matthew agreed, touching the top of the girl's head. "And that you are."

"And you'd have a dog if you'd just get one." Carrie's eyes were huge and fairly puppy-like as she regarded him.

Natalie suspected Matthew's big house would be filled with the sound of barking before long. Carrie seemed to have a way of getting people to do what she wanted with a flash of her big brown eyes and precious smile.

After all, Natalie was at Matthew's house, and who would have ever thought that possible?

CHAPTER NINE

"How's OUR GIRL this morning?"

Natalie jumped at the sound of Matthew's voice behind her. Straightening from where she'd been examining the tiny baby in the special ICU bassinette, she faced him.

"So far, so good."

"Her color is good."

It was. The baby's skin was a nice pink. If everything held course, they'd start removing some of the lines later today, and continue to monitor the baby's progress closely over the next several days.

"Thank you for your help with her."

He gave a half-smile. "You'd have gotten the valves to work if I hadn't been there."

He was right. She wouldn't have stopped until she'd done all she could for the baby. He'd just made it easier.

And taught her a new technique.

Had they not had an affair, she might have liked him.

He smiled at her and her heart fluttered.

Ha. Part of her still liked him.

A lot.

Good thing there was that part of her that didn't like him, else she might be in trouble for having inappropriate thoughts about her boss. Her boss whom she'd slept with before he was her boss, and before she'd known what he was doing for a little girl who could have easily ended up in foster care, as Natalie had.

Not wanting to have empathetic thoughts about him, she turned back to the baby, taking another listen to her tiny heart.

"Thank you for going with Carrie and me last night."

"I shouldn't have." Her response was automatic, the truth, but a part of her didn't regret having gone, having seen that uncertain part of him that wanted to do right by Carrie so desperately, yet didn't seem to know quite how.

"I didn't expect you to," he admitted from where he stood next to the bassinette.

"She's hard to say no to."

He gave a low laugh. "Tell me about it. I'm going to have to learn, though, or I'll have her spoiled rotten. It's so difficult not to give her everything she wants to try to make up for all she's dealing with."

Natalie could only imagine. She barely knew the child and she'd found herself drifting off to sleep thinking about puppies.

"Including getting stuck with me."

"She seems to be a good kid, overall," Natalie mused.

"She is. The best. She's..." His voice trailed off. "Sorry, I know you don't want to hear about Carrie. Or anything to do with my personal life. Sorry she roped you into last night, but I do appreciate your going with us."

Natalie swallowed the lump in her throat. Yeah, she shouldn't want to hear anything about Carrie or his personal life, but part of her was sorely disappointed he'd stopped talking, that he'd felt the need to.

Which was ridiculous. She understood and embraced that need to halt anything even slightly personal between them. It was how it needed to be.

Just as she needed to put some distance between them because last night had her all mixed up.

"Have you made a decision about the Harris case?"

His question jolted her back to reality. Focusing on the baby rather than looking up at him, Natalie nodded. "I'm going to operate."

"I'd like to be in surgery with you."

She'd thought he might. Perhaps that had been part of her hesitation in making the decision, but her window of opportunity was quickly passing. If the Harris baby was going to have her vessels repaired in utero and have time to heal prior to entering this world, the operation had to take place soon.

"You planning to take over again?"

His gaze narrowed. "Is that how you saw what happened?"

No, it wasn't. Her comment had been unfair and unwarranted. Matthew had been nothing but kind since his arrival in Memphis. So why had she snapped at him?

She knew why. The same reason her insides were twisted into knots. Last night—seeing him vulnerable when she'd thought him invincible, seeing him giving up so much to try to take care of his best friend's daughter.

And then there was Miami.

She couldn't look at him and not remember how his lips had felt against her body, how his body had felt against hers, how they'd laughed together, played together, how she'd let loose and relaxed with him because she'd thought she'd never see him again.

That was the reason she'd been so relaxed with him, wasn't it?

Yet here he was in Memphis.

Driving her crazy. Mentally, emotionally, physically.

"You can do as you please," she assured, trying not to let too much of her unease come through. "It's not as if I have the authority to say no."

She made the mistake of looking up, catching his light blue gaze darkening as he studied her.

"Is there someone you'd rather have in this particular surgery with you than the surgeon on staff who has the most in-utero surgical experience?"

She took a deep breath, then glanced beyond him to make sure no one was near enough to overhear their conversation.

"Of course I don't want you in surgery with me." Only, she did. Which annoyed her all the more. Then again, she'd admired his skills long before she knew just how far they extended.

"Explain."

"We had sex," she whispered.

"So what?" He kept his voice low. "That has nothing to do with this."

"It has everything to do with this," she assured. "If I'd known there was even the slightest possibility that I'd someday work with you, we never would have."

With one last look at the baby, she walked away, ducked into a dictation room for a moment's privacy to calm her racing heart. She should have known Matthew would follow her.

"Our having sex is in the past," he said matter-of-factly, filling the doorway to the small closet-like room. "We can't change the past. But how we proceed in the future is something we do have control over. I let you dictate the animosity between us from the moment I arrived on the Memphis scene because I agreed that keeping our distance was for the best. But I was wrong. The reality is, we can't keep enough distance to avoid the truth."

"What truth?"

He raked his fingers through his dark hair. "You want me."

Three simple words spoken softly but they echoed around the tiny room.

"You're mistaken," she denied.

"You want me as much as I want you," he clarified, causing her breath to lodge in her throat. "You want to know if we made love again if it would be as intense as in Miami."

"You're crazy." Natalie shook her head. She didn't want to know that. If it was she'd never be able to maintain a professional relationship with him.

She had to maintain a professional relationship with him.

"But my working here complicates things. My being your boss complicates things. I get that. Especially as making this cardiology program everything it can be is important to me." He took a long breath, raked his fingers through his hair again. "I won't let you or anyone keep that from happening. I need this position to work. For my sake and for Carrie's."

Natalie winced.

"If you think it's impossible to work with me because of our physical attraction then we need to figure this out before it compromises the program."

"I'd never do anything to compromise the program or any patient," she adamantly denied, ignoring the rest of what he said. She'd devoted her professional life to Memphis Children's Hospital. How could he question her loyalty?

"Great," he said as if he'd just won a major argument, his entire demeanor relaxing and an easy smile flashing across his handsome face. "Then you'll be fine with the fact that I'm assisting on your surgery this afternoon on the Givens baby, who's being flown in right now." His expression grew a little more serious. "I will also be in on the Harris case."

Natalie could almost forget that Matthew stood across the operating table from her. Almost.

Okay, so not really.

Thus far, he had assisted, but otherwise hadn't pushed for a more controlling role in the Givens baby's surgery.

Andy Givens had been born in an outlying community hospital that morning and had quickly gotten into distress and been transported via helicopter to Memphis Children's.

Being the surgeon on call that day, Natalie had been assigned the case and had shifted her clinic schedule to perform the repair of the baby's tiny valve and vessels.

With Matthew working right along beside her.

It would be easy to get distracted by the efficient movements of his hands, of the skill with which he worked, but she kept her focus on the repairs rather than where Matthew worked on the baby's tiny heart simultaneously via the robotic device that allowed such fine manipulation.

When they'd finished, Natalie scrubbed her hands, ignoring that Matthew joined her. He made a few comments, but she brushed them off.

Surgery with him was getting to her. Spending time with him was getting to her. His earlier claims were getting to her.

She didn't want anything about him to get to her.

Her insides felt raw, her mind raced, her heart ached. She needed to be alone, to assimilate the evening's events. The last thing she wanted was to get caught in conversation with him, but he seemed to have other ideas as he fell into step beside her. "You okay?"

"Ecstatic."

"No regrets?"

Without slowing her pace, she cut her gaze toward him. "Regarding?"

"My being in there with you."

"It's not what I would have chosen, but everything seems to have gone well, so..." She let her voice trail off as she punched the elevator call button.

"Is my being in surgery with you that big of a problem, Natalie?" he asked as they stepped into the empty elevator.

She pressed the button for the floor where her office was located and wished he'd push another button indicating he was headed to another floor. Any floor but hers. Which wouldn't make sense since his office was located down the hallway from hers.

Staring at the elevator floor indicator and wishing it would hurry up, Natalie said, "The surgery went well. That's what's important."

The elevator dinged then the door slid open. Matthew stood back, letting Natalie exit first. Not that he had a long wait—she practically leapt out. They headed down a long hallway and entered the cardiology center, where an office complex was located. It being late in the evening, the corridor to their offices was eerily silent, and to get to his office they had to walk past hers first.

Sensing Matthew standing behind her, she punched in the security code that would unlock her office, and when the door clicked open she drew in a deep breath.

"You planning to stay here tonight?"

Without turning to face him, she nodded. "I'm on call, so I planned on going to the computer lab to work on the Harris case. Plus, I want to be close if there are any changes on the Givens baby."

"Call if you need me."

A million thoughts ran through her mind. None of which had anything to do with her cases. Heat flooded her and she was glad he couldn't see her face. But he must have sensed what was on her mind, because when he spoke his voice was low.

"It's moments like these where I have to remind myself that I promised to leave you alone on a personal level, because right then I almost turned you to face me, Natalie."

Her breath caught and she squeezed her eyes shut as if that would somehow stop the onslaught of emotions hitting her.

"For the record, I don't find not touching you easy."

Neither did she, which was why it was so important they keep a distance.

His words from before struck her. Was he right? Was there no distance great enough to stop her from wanting him?

She *did* want him, hadn't stopped wanting him. He was here, right behind her, alone in this private section of the hospital office complex. All she had to do was turn, reach out and touch him, and…and then what?

Her heart pounded in her chest. Her hand fell from the code pad and she turned, met his pale eyes.

He stared at her, seeing what she wasn't sure because she couldn't label the confusion swirling within her. She wanted him to disappear, to have never met him, for him to be back in Boston performing his miraculous surgeries.

But even more she wanted him to touch her, to take charge and take what he wanted—what she wanted.

So why wasn't she reaching out to touch him?

Because if she touched him she had to acknowledge that everything he said was true, that maybe she couldn't work with him day after day and ignore what was between them. Because pretending she didn't want him, that Miami had been one big mistake, was a lot easier than acknowledging he was a part of her daily life, and that scared her.

Her lips parted. To say what, she wasn't sure, just that so much emotion churned within her she needed to let it out somehow. Or maybe she'd been offering a subconscious invitation.

Regardless, Matthew's gaze didn't soften—instead it took on that dark and dangerous look that made her wonder how she'd ever thought him vulnerable the night before.

"Goodnight, Natalie," he said. "Great job in surgery today. If there are any unexpected changes, let me know."

With that, he opened her office door, practically pushed her inside and walked away without a backward glance.

Dr Luiz's retirement party was a huge success. The hospital's CEO had given quite the toast to the man early on in the evening. Hospital staff, along with VIP members of the medical community and from Memphis's social and political scene, had been slapping the retiring doctor on the back all evening, and still came up to do so every so often.

At the moment, a couple had interrupted Matthew's conversation with the older surgeon to tell him how missed he would be at the hospital. Matthew let Dr. Luiz explain that he was only semi-retiring and would still be around the hospital, just significantly scaling back on his duties and no longer overseeing the department.

His semi-retirement was one of the things that made the position work for Matthew. With Dr. Luiz still there part-time and with a second-in-command of Natalie's caliber, Matthew's workload wasn't near as heavy as in Boston. Which gave him more time to spend with Carrie, for them to figure out this new life of theirs.

Maybe he'd get used to the idea of working less and parenting more. Maybe he'd get better at it. Hopefully. His sister had Carrie tonight, and the little girl would have a good time with her cousins. Would be in a home where the adult in the household knew what she was doing.

Something Matthew wondered if he'd ever figure out.

The couple were still chatting with Dr Luiz, and Matthew spent the time glancing around the crowd, wondering if Natalie was there yet. Sweet and sassy Natalie, who was determined to keep him at arms' length. Which he should be grateful for. He didn't need to risk anything—anyone—messing up his new life in Memphis.

He'd gotten a whole lot wrong over the past few months, but moving to Memphis had been right—the best decision he'd made in a long time.

There had only been one negative: Natalie and their strained working relationship.

If he'd known there was even the slightest possibility Memphis Children's would come through, he'd never have given in to his desire for her.

At least, he'd like to think he wouldn't have.

There was something about her that messed with his head, so who knew if in sunny Miami, away from all the stresses of his life, he'd have been able to resist the temptation she'd presented with her quick smile and desire-filled eyes?

He missed that Natalie. The one who had looked at him with delight, touched him with longing, carried on long, flirty conversations with him and shared nights that had passed much too quickly.

Maybe that was part of him missing his old life, the life where he'd been free to have as many affairs as he wanted, where he'd been free to focus on his work. Where he hadn't had to second-guess every decision he made and how it would impact a child.

Or maybe it was just Natalie.

Searching the crowded ballroom, he had no difficulty spotting her. She stood out in any room, but looked particularly lovely tonight. She wore a figure-hugging black dress that accentuated her rocking body. Her hair was down—something he hadn't seen since Florida, as she always kept it pulled up at the hospital. Memories of running his fingers through those locks haunted him, making him long to cross the room and touch the silky strands.

To think his fascination was anything other than unique to her was foolish. No woman from his past had monopolized his thoughts, his desires, the way Natalie did.

"Ah, Dr. Sterling is here."

Apparently the couple had moved on without Matthew noticing and the guest of honor's gaze had followed his.

He didn't turn to meet Dr. Luiz's eyes. No need. The man wasn't stupid and had made several comments over the past few weeks that let Matthew know he might not know details, but he knew something was up.

"She is," Matthew agreed. In her scrubs, hair pulled up and no make-up, Natalie was gorgeous. Tonight, dressed to shine, she should have been featured in one of the fashion magazines Carrie loved to look at.

"I have to admit," the older man said from beside Matthew, "I thought she'd have warmed to you by now."

"She may never warm to me. I took what she saw as hers."

"That's not it and we both know it."

His confident tone had Matthew's gaze dragging off Natalie and glancing toward the astute older man.

"I've known her for a decade and have never seen Natalie react to anyone the way she does to you. You agitate her."

"Agitation's not a good thing."

"Matter of opinion, but I'd say it's not a bad thing."

Matthew's gaze narrowed on the man he greatly respected. "Our opinions differ on that. She resents me, and you, too, for what she sees as a direct betrayal and slap in her face career-wise in that she didn't get to take over the department."

"I'd put money on the fact that her agitation with you has nothing to do with anything that's happened in Memphis."

Which implied the man suspected something had happened *before* his arrival in Memphis.

"I didn't do anything in Miami to make Natalie dislike me, if that's what you're implying."

"I didn't say she disliked you." The man's brow furrowed. "Unlike the idiot who is falling all over himself in front of her in hopes she'll beg him back."

Matthew's gaze returned to Natalie to see a tall, slim, suited man fawning over her. Natalie's expression wasn't pleasant, but it also held enough emotion to give away that the man wasn't a casual acquaintance. Even without Dr. Luiz's comment, Matthew would have known the guy had to be her ex.

The one whom she'd lived with for a couple of years.

A man who'd shared her life, her bed, her body.

A man who was reaching for her hand even as Matthew watched.

Green acid gurgled within him, and it had nothing to do with anything he'd eaten and everything to do with the man touching Natalie.

The man—*what had his name been?*—lifted her hand and pressed a kiss there. The acid in

Matthew's belly erupted into full-blown volcanic burn.

His vision blurred.

Did the fool think he could have her back?

Not that Matthew had any say in the matter, but Natalie was smarter than to take back a man who'd cheated.

Only, she wasn't telling the guy who still held her hand to get lost, and Matthew knew firsthand that she had no problems whatsoever with saying those words.

CHAPTER TEN

"You're looking especially beautiful tonight, Nat."

Before Natalie realized what Jonathan was doing, he'd grabbed her hand and kissed it in what he clearly hoped would appear as charming.

Natalie was not charmed.

Shock reverberated through her. Wasn't he engaged to the woman he'd been cheating with, or had her friends been mistaken?

Either way, Natalie wanted nothing to do with him, and attempted to jerk her hand free, but his hold tightened. "I can't say it's nice to see you," she said.

His smooth smile didn't waver and neither did his hold. "Nat, Nat, Nat. You aren't still bitter about what happened?"

"No." She wasn't bitter. "Bitterness would imply I care. We both know that you screwing around on me did me a big favor. Let my hand go."

"Ouch!" he exclaimed, but didn't look as if Natalie's words fazed him. Instead of letting go of her hand, he brought it to his lips again and pressed another kiss to her fingertips. "I miss you and that sharp wit of yours."

Stunned by his public show of affection when they really hadn't been into a lot of PDA when they were together, she stared at him in confusion, and more than a little irritation.

"You have to be kidding me. Aren't you and what's-her-name engaged? I know I saw her with you earlier. Why are you even over here talking to me? You should be with her."

He tsked. "You shouldn't believe everything you hear."

"You aren't engaged?"

His gaze didn't quite meet hers; instead he studied where he held her hand. "I didn't say that."

Natalie rolled her eyes and managed to pull her hand free.

"Tell me you don't miss me." He took a step toward her and Natalie automatically took a step back.

"That you don't come home," he continued,

stepping closer yet again, "and wish I was there in our bed."

"Ask me to do something difficult because this one is way too easy." She lifted her chin a little, looked him square in the eyes, and said, "I don't miss you, and I'm glad you're not in my bed."

"I don't believe you." His utter arrogance amazed Natalie. How had she not realized what a smug idiot he was?

"I don't care what you believe. Not anymore." She wasn't sure she ever had. Which was sad. She'd lived with him, had sex with him, hoped he'd be the one to love her and never leave her. She had cared about him once upon a time.

"You don't miss our nights together?" He loomed, his expression sneering, suggestive, as if he really believed her to be pining for him to return. "Aren't you lonely, Natalie? Missing a man's touch?"

When had he backed her into a corner? And how had he done so without her realizing? She opened her mouth to tell him what a fool he was and to push past him, but before she could someone answered for her.

"Not in the slightest."

Natalie jumped at the male voice, at the strong

hand that slid around her waist and settled possessively on her low back as Matthew's body inserted itself between her and Jonathan.

"I assure you she's not lonely," he continued, donning a smug look of his own. "But then, only a fool would believe a woman as beautiful and passionate as Natalie would be lonely."

Natalie didn't know whether to slap Matthew or to hug him. Hug him because Jonathan's smugness had completely vanished. Slap him because they were in a room full of their peers and she'd just as soon no one wondered what was up with her and her sexy new heart surgeon boss.

Glancing around the room, she thought it didn't seem anyone was paying the slightest attention. Plus, Jonathan had backed them to where they were semi-blocked from most of the other guests.

She should be grateful Matthew hadn't added "or missing a man's touch".

Then again, that wouldn't have been true because she *had* been missing a man's touch. Just not Jonathan's. She missed Matthew. His smile. His conversations. His kisses. His touch.

Even now his fingers burned through the thin material of her dress and scorched her back, making her want to arch into him, making her want to forget all the reasons why anything other than a purely professional relationship between them was a very bad idea.

"And you are?" Jonathan's expression was snide as he visually measured Natalie's rescuer.

Resisting the urge to pull away from Matthew, Natalie smiled instead and introduced the only two men she'd ever been intimate with. *How weird was that?*

"You're Natalie's new boss?" Jonathan's gaze bounced back and forth between them. His grin was vicious. "Having to resort to sleeping your way to the top now? First passed over for another woman, and just a few months later passed over for another heart surgeon." He gave a low laugh. "Not being quite good enough yet again has to sting, Natalie. Especially when you worked so hard for this."

His words were meant to hurt. Natalie knew that. She tried not to let them, but they reached their mark. Why had she ever shared her past hurts, her future aspirations with this buffoon?

"Dr Coleman deserved the position." Oh, how it hurt to say that out loud. "His credentials are excellent." They were. "Memphis Children's is lucky to have a doctor of his caliber join our staff."

Jonathan laughed. "You forget I lived with you for over two years and know you better than anyone," he reminded. "All your long hours being for nothing must kill you."

It did.

"My work wasn't for nothing. I saved lives, Jonathan. Something you have no concept of."

"You sound so altruistic," he sneered.

Matthew's body tensed and Natalie continued, trying to diffuse the situation. The last thing she wanted was a scene at Dr. Luiz's party. "You must not have been paying attention all those years you claim to have gotten to know me." She cast what she hoped was a look of appreciation toward Matthew. "I've always admired Matthew's work and look forward to learning all I can from working with someone of his talent."

"Right. This guy comes along and you're suddenly okay with not getting the position you've been busting your butt for since the beginning?" He turned to Matthew. "Better watch out, buddy. Her career means everything to her and you got in the way. You know that old saying about keeping your friends close and your enemies closer? You might be enjoying being in my old bed, but I'd watch my back if I were you."

Matthew, who'd been watching their exchange, had that dark and dangerous expression he wore so well. "I'm not worried."

His look said Jonathan would be wise to be worried, though.

"Pity," Jonathan mocked, getting in his parting shot. "You should be."

Natalie stared at the retreating back of her ex and shook her head. How could she have ever had a relationship with such a sleazeball? And she was *so* replacing her bedroom furniture ASAP.

"Real winner there, Natalie."

Like she needed him to tell her that.

"Yeah, I can really pick them, can't I?" She gave him a pointed look. "Why did you interrupt?"

"I didn't like how he was crowding you into a corner."

Neither had she, but she lifted her chin and glared at Matthew. "I can take care of myself."

"Apparently. I'll be sure to wear chain mail beneath my scrubs."

"You're too funny." Her heart pounded. "It was none of your business."

"I felt as if it was. I really didn't like how he was looking at you." Matthew's eyes searched hers. "How he kissed your hand and wouldn't let go."

"It wasn't anything to do with you," she reminded, feeling way more crowded than she previously had. But in a different way. Matthew made her feel...breathless.

Watching her for a few long moments, his pale blue eyes softened and he said, "Dance with me, Natalie."

Where had his invitation come from?

"I thought you agreed that we needed to keep things professional between us?"

"Dr Luiz thinks you don't like me, that there is animosity between us. If he's picked up on it, then others may have. We need to put on a united front. For the department," he added when she readied to argue. "Besides, we danced together in Miami, so this really isn't that big of a deal."

Touching Matthew, dancing with him, would be a very big deal.

"Dancing in Miami was different."

"Everything in Miami was different."

She nodded, forced herself to look away. Everything *had* been different. He'd been a stranger, someone she was free to be silly with, someone she was never supposed to see again, someone who wouldn't interfere with her life or her career goals.

Now he was her boss, had a child, and was someone she saw almost daily.

"Dr Luiz suspects something happened between us."

She thought so, too. "Probably."

"You don't sound upset. Did you say something to him?"

She gave a horrified look. "Why would I do that? Besides, why does it have to be me who said something? Maybe it was something you said."

"Maybe," he admitted, his gaze going off to where Jonathan had rejoined the woman he'd come with.

Poor girl.

"I wanted to punch him when he kissed your hand."

Shocked, Natalie shot her gaze to Matthew. "You're too talented a surgeon to risk anything that stupid. He's not worth messing up your hands. It'd be a shame if you couldn't operate."

The dark color to Matthew's face morphed into a full-blown smile. "Always thinking work, Natalie?"

She didn't respond.

"I was saying I wanted to defend your honor, admitting to being jealous, and your response is that I should protect my surgeon hands at all cost?"

Warmth at his admission spread through Natalie and she fought melting against him.

Monica's and Suzie's comments about making him jealous popped into her mind. She hadn't been trying to do that, especially not with Jonathan. They'd have a field day with that one.

Still, she needed to keep focused on what was important, on what her real goals were.

"Admitting to jealousy is personal, Matthew. We only have a professional relationship, remember?"

"I keep forgetting."

Needing to put a sharp halt to that line of thinking, Natalie asked, "Where's Carrie?"

"Spending the night at my sister's. I'm a single man tonight. Home alone. You could come over, keep me from getting lonely."

Natalie ignored the single man part, the being home alone part, the coming over part, the keeping him from getting lonely part, because she couldn't let herself think about why he'd tell her those things. She just couldn't.

Even not allowing herself to think on those things had her heart-rate kicking up several notches.

"You have a sister?" He'd mentioned her before, but focusing in on that comment seemed the safest route.

He laughed. "You make it sound as if I must have come from a test tube. You mentioned your parents were killed in an automobile accident, but don't *you* have other family?"

She so wasn't going to go there. Not with Matthew. Not with anyone. She didn't talk about her sordid foster life prior to the McCulloughs taking her in.

"Does your sister live close?"

Letting it slide that she had answered his question with one of her own, he nodded. "About a twenty-minute drive from the hospital. She's just down the street from my mother. It's great being near them."

"Why have I never read that you were from Memphis?"

"If you read anything about my background, which is unlikely, it would have said I was from

Arkansas. I grew up in a small town just over the state line. Until the past month, I've never technically lived in Memphis or Tennessee."

"I see."

"I'm not sure you do."

Her gaze met his and she saw things that would be better not seen.

Because she saw what he'd admitted to—jealousy, possessiveness, desire, longing.

She'd told him he had no right to feel those things, yet she'd never stopped feeling desire for him. Longing for him.

Lord help her if he ever showed up with another woman; she'd feel possessive, jealous.

Which was ridiculous. She should not want Matthew.

He'd been a fling.

He'd taken her job.

She was pretty sure spending time with him would destroy everything she held dear.

Yet she wanted him anyway.

"You were right to say no to dancing with me, Natalie." He looked at her as if he were going to gobble her up.

She was probably looking at him as if she wanted him to.

"Why's that?"

"Because the moment your body was next to mine everyone in the room would have known how much I want you. I've never been good at pretense or games, and denying whatever this is between us is getting more and more difficult."

She glanced away, not sure what to say. She wanted him, too, but admitting that sure wasn't on the tip of her tongue.

"This whole thing is impossible."

"What thing?" he asked.

"You being here. You working at my hospital. You. Just everything about you."

He studied her, then, grinning, asked, "Do I agitate you?"

Why was he grinning? What was up with his question? "What?"

"You sound agitated."

She frowned. Had he lost his mind? "I am beyond agitated. You annoy me no end. Go away."

But rather than him looking hurt or offended, Matthew's grin widened. "You want to get out of here with me?"

Had he not heard a word of what she'd said? "No."

"That's not what I meant. Well, that always seems to be in the background of what I'm feeling where you're concerned, but I was thinking more along the lines of going somewhere to get a cup of coffee and talk. This," he gestured around the party in full swing, "isn't really my scene."

Hers neither. She'd talked with the board members and their significant others, had put in an appearance because she respected and adored Dr. Luiz, even if she hadn't quite forgiven him. She was ready to leave. But with Matthew?

Get a cup of coffee and talk. It sounded so innocent.

So tempting.

"Fine. Coffee. Talk. Nothing else."

But if it really was innocent, if she really believed she was just going for coffee and talk, why did every warning bell in Natalie's head sound?

CHAPTER ELEVEN

MATTHEW LET NATALIE make the rounds saying her farewells to several of their colleagues, to Dr. Luiz and his wife. He waited for her to leave, alone, kept an eye on her bozo ex to make sure the idiot didn't follow, and within fifteen minutes made his own farewell rounds and left the party still in full swing.

He half expected Natalie to have changed her mind, for her to not be sitting in the coffee shop where they'd agreed to meet. It didn't take a genius to see how torn she was about him.

That he understood.

There was a lot about her that had his insides torn as well. But having seen her ex pawing at her seemed to have tossed out his common sense and good intentions.

When he arrived at the coffee shop, she was sipping on a cup of something hot and reading on her phone. To the casual observer, she looked calm. Matthew wasn't a casual observer. He noticed the little tremor in the hand that held her phone, the way she moistened her lips several times, the way her eyes closed and she appeared to be praying.

For what? For strength to tell him to get lost? For him not to stand her up? Or maybe the opposite; maybe it would be easier if he just turned and left, giving her something else to hold against him?

Something shifted inside his chest. Something monumental.

All because of this woman.

He wanted her.

At the moment, fighting the way she made him feel seemed ridiculous.

Which was, itself, crazy. Even if he could convince Natalie they weren't toying with insanity and risking their careers to spend the night together, even if he could convince her to say yes, how would they react to each other on Monday?

Was it possible that if they had sex again it would dampen the fire burning between them? That maybe they could move on and have a truly professional relationship?

Could he risk everything to find out?

Carrie was adjusting to Memphis so well, loved being near Matthew's family. No wonder, when he was such a screw-up stand-in parent and his family had stepped in and pulled the child into their fold. His sister had wanted Carrie to spend the night with her two girls. They'd been headed to a movie then having a girls' slumber party. Carrie was no doubt having a blast with five-year-old Mandy and three-year-old Liz.

Matthew wanted to have the time of *his* life.

With Natalie.

What would one night hurt?

Perhaps sensing him watching her, she glanced up from her phone and spotted him, looking a little leery, like she wasn't sure if she was glad he was there or not. Still, she managed a soft smile, and Matthew knew he was a goner.

Perhaps he'd been a goner from the moment he'd noticed her in the airport and not been able to get her out of his brain since.

Either way, he wanted her, knew she wanted him.

He intended to have her.

Natalie resisted the urge to squirm. Matthew was looking at her oddly. Like he wanted to gobble her up in one swift bite and slay dragons for her all at the same time.

It was a heady, very confusing expression, and her head spun as she watched him approach her table.

Not bothering with ordering a coffee of his own, he came over, sat down and smiled a smile that didn't ease the nervous tension running through her.

If anything, more tension thrummed to life.

"What?" she asked, setting her phone on the table. She'd read the same first line of the article she'd been trying to read a dozen times and still couldn't tell what it said.

Why was she staring into his smiling face, thinking he was too handsome to be real, and recalling that she'd held that face, kissed that face, woken up to that face just a couple of months before?

"Thinking how lucky I am that you're really here. I wasn't sure you would be."

Her nervousness mounting, Natalie rolled her eyes. "Cut it with the corny comments."

"Nothing corny about telling a beautiful woman you appreciate being with her."

Heat flooded her cheeks. They shouldn't be here. Shouldn't be having this conversation. "What are we doing, Matthew?"

His pale blue eyes twinkled. "Having coffee?"

"You don't have coffee."

He glanced down in front of him at the empty table as if her announcement was news to him. "Would it make you feel better if I ordered a drink?"

Her heart beat wildly in her chest, pounding against her ribcage, beating her logic into submission. "This is crazy."

He leaned across the table, his gaze holding hers with an intensity that made breathing difficult. "Wasting time is always crazy. A very wise woman pointed that out to me in Miami not so long ago."

Her gaze dropped to his lips. To his magical, glorious lips that felt so good against hers. Lips that had just implied they were wasting precious time when they could be... Natalie lifted her gaze back to his, but realized that didn't help.

She knew what he was saying, what he wanted.

The same thing she wanted.

The same reason those warning bells had gone off when she'd agreed to meet him for coffee. Because she wanted him.

Felt as if she'd always wanted him.

He wanted her, too. He was using those hypnotic eyes to will her to cut to the chase and admit what she was feeling.

Why not? a little voice asked. Why not give in to his temptation and let him do marvelous things to her body? Nothing would be different. They'd had sex in the past. What would one more night hurt?

Maybe another night would even help. Maybe having sex with Matthew in Memphis wouldn't be nearly as good as she thought having sex with him in Florida had been.

"I want to take you home, Natalie."

Her insides melted.

"To spend the entire night making love to you. In *my* bed."

Visions of his bedroom, of his big bed, flashed into her mind. Visions of her, of him, naked, their bodies locked together in his massive bed.

Her memories were playing tricks on her, right? Miami hadn't really been as magical as her mind made it out to be. He hadn't really made her body sing song after glorious song.

"Let me make love to you, Natalie."

Who was she to deny him?

After all, she was merely mortal, not some super-heroic woman. Who could resist his out-of-this-world allure?

Yeah, logic had been pulverized, because, rather than reminding him of all the reasons they shouldn't, she stood and tossed the remainder of her drink into the closest trash bin.

"Time's wasting," she reminded when Matthew still sat at the table, watching her every move. "You coming?"

Natalie woke with a start, realized she wasn't in her bed and pulled the covers up higher over her bare breasts.

Her bare everything.

Because she was naked and in Matthew's bed. In Matthew's house.

In Memphis.

She turned her head, stared at the sleeping man next to her and fought a million emotions.

He was so darn good-looking and so sexually gifted that it was no wonder she'd ended up back in bed with him.

It was more than that.

He was more than that.

Her mind hadn't been playing tricks on her. If anything, Matthew had been better than she recalled. Had developed even more superpowers to reach inside her body and melt every single cell into ooey, gooey, orgasmic, floating nothingness.

Who knew sex could be like that? That a

woman could be so in tune with a man that his every move felt an extension of her own being?

Unable to resist, she touched him, tracing over the strong lines of his face.

Immediately his eyes opened, their pale depths focusing on her, and he smiled. "You really here or am I dreaming?"

She knew what he meant. None of this seemed real. The night before had seemed as something from a fantasy, not real life.

Because when Matthew had made love to her the first time last night there had been an intensity, a fervor, that surpassed anything they'd experienced in Florida.

It had been as if he'd been claiming her as his own, his body telling her she was his, and no time, distance or anything else would change that.

The second time there had been a sweetness, a tenderness mixed in with his urgency and passion. Every touch had been all about her, about giving pleasure, and pulling every single nerve ending to maximum sensory overload.

He had.

Dear, sweet heaven, what this man had done to her body.

He captured her fingers within his, brought

them to his lips and pressed a kiss to their tips. "Real."

She bit the inside of her lower lip. This was real.

She was in bed with Matthew. Her boss.

She knew better, knew how risky doing something so stupid was. Yet with Matthew, she seemed unable to heed logic.

"You're thinking too much, Natalie. You have a nasty habit of doing that."

"Sorry," she said, shrugging her shoulders and realizing she'd caused the covers to slip and expose the upper swell of her breasts. "Sorry," she repeated, tugging on the covers.

"Don't be. Embrace this the way you did in Miami."

"This was supposed to have ended in Miami," she reminded him.

"But it didn't."

"No," she admitted. Nothing had ended in Miami. Even before he'd arrived in Memphis, she'd not been able to stop thinking about him, wondering what would have happened if she'd told him she wanted to see him again. "It's not good that we didn't end it."

He was silent a moment, then asked, "Because of work?"

"You're my boss," she reminded. "We both know if it came down to having to let one of us go that I'd be the one ousted."

"I'd never use our relationship against you."

"I didn't say you would. If things didn't work and got nasty between us, you wouldn't have to say anything. The hospital board could opt to take matters into their own hands."

"There's no policy against our being together, Natalie."

"I don't think they'd encourage us to be in your bed, risking possible drama down the road."

"Maybe not, but we're good together. Unlike anything I've ever known. You feel it, too." In some ways what he was saying was magic to her ears. In others, he scared her. "Neither of us is into drama," he pointed out. "I don't see either of us letting our physical relationship interfere with our work."

She wanted to believe what he was saying.

"I'd like to do this again," he admitted, lacing his fingers with hers.

"As in?"

"I want to keep having sex with you."

Keep having sex with Matthew. It sounded

so simple, so tempting. Yet, what was he really saying?

"Do you mean as in us dating?" she asked.

"I'm not looking for anything long-term, but yes, I'd like to date you."

He sounded as surprised at his admission as Natalie felt.

"I'm not good at dating." Just look at how her relationship with Jonathan had ended.

"Because you haven't dated *me*."

Part of her wanted to snort at his arrogance, but how could she scoff when he was right?

"I wasn't the only one who only wanted three days in Miami and said there couldn't be anything beyond that," she reminded him. "I assume your reasons had to do with Carrie."

That had him pausing, raking his fingers through his hair, then pulling her to him. Inches separated their faces as he held her close. "Carrie thinks you're cool."

Carrie had thought she was cool?

"She's a great kid," he continued, as if he needed to sell her on the little girl.

"She is, but…" Natalie took a deep breath. "What if our being involved is a problem? What then?"

"Do you overanalyze everything?"

"Yes. It's what a good heart surgeon and researcher does."

"True, but there are times when you have to just trust your gut instinct."

"If I trusted my gut instinct I wouldn't be in your bed," she admitted rather bluntly.

"Fine, don't trust your gut instinct," he quickly corrected, not looking in the slightest deterred. He rolled, pinning her beneath him, but keeping his weight to where if she wanted to get free she could easily do so. He brushed the tip of his nose against hers. "Trust in me, Natalie."

His plea sounded so simple, yet nothing could be less true. Everything about her spending time with Matthew was complicated, and trusting him? Ha! How could she when not only would her personal life be on the line, but also her professional one?

"Trust in this." He kissed her. Softly, slowly, tenderly.

His lips felt so good on hers, so perfect.

She should tell him to stop, to not further muddy her mind with lust. But she didn't want him to stop. She just wanted to feel, to squeeze every precious memory from the moment.

To give in to the lust.

It *was* just lust she was feeling, right?

"Promise you'll give us a chance," he whispered against her lips, pausing to drop another lingering kiss against her mouth.

She blinked up at him. "Are you using sex to seduce me into agreeing to continue to have sex with you?"

He chuckled. "I want you, Natalie. I'll use whatever means necessary to convince you to agree with me."

He set about doing just that, loving her so intently that Natalie was left gasping for air and wondering how she'd ever thought she could deny him anything.

Once they got out of bed, Matthew made Natalie breakfast, then drove her to her apartment to let her shower and change prior to their both going to the hospital, where they rounded on their patients and took care of paperwork. When done, Natalie headed to the cardiac computer lab to review the Harris case yet again.

Which was where Matthew found her.

"Tuesday morning would be a great day to schedule this."

Glancing up from the computer screen, Natalie caught her breath at the vision of him leaning against the door jamb.

Her body had been all tangled up with his just hours before.

Lucky her. Only… No, she wasn't going to think about that. Not right now. No doubt later logic would regain its strength and take the reins back, but for now she was going to pretend logic didn't exist, had never existed.

She arched a brow. "You're available that morning?"

Surprise at her comment lit in his eyes. Pleased surprise. "The first surgery of its kind performed at this hospital? I'd clear my schedule."

She nodded. "The possibilities of where this could take treatments for transposed vessels is exciting, isn't it?"

"Very. Walk me through the case."

Natalie ran through the computer simulation, just as she'd done dozens of times before. Only this time Matthew was with her, offering praise, making suggestions, discussing possible scenarios that could come up and how they'd respond.

Natalie made mental notes, knew she'd be writing them down later, would be going back through the simulation at least a dozen times more prior to putting Delaine Harris on the operating table to repair her baby's heart.

So many things could go wrong.

So many things could go right.

If she failed, Delaine's baby would face even greater health issues than she would have had they waited until she was born. There was a risk the procedure could force her baby to be born much too soon.

If she succeeded, Delaine's baby would never be a "blue baby", would be able to go home with her parents much sooner, would have a much stronger heart due to the healing that would take place while she was still growing inside her mother, would have less complications later in life.

If what Natalie and several of her colleagues believed was true, the overall benefits of doing the repairs while the baby was still in utero rather than waiting until after birth far outweighed the risks.

But there were always things that came up that one wasn't expecting. Which was why she kept running through the computer simulations, trying to plan for anything unexpected.

Matthew had been pioneering new pediatric heart surgery techniques for years. She'd draw on his experience, and would welcome his assistance. Because of Delaine and her baby, not because she'd had sex with him again.

Phenomenal, out-of-this-world sex.

Last night and again that morning.

Everything seemed wonderful, but Natalie knew it was only a ruse, that this euphoria wouldn't last, and that when it came to an end she'd be the one hurt.

Still, it would take a stronger woman than she was to withstand the power in his blue gaze.

As head of the department, Matthew had already familiarized himself with the Harris case and Natalie's innovative treatment plan. He let her walk him through the simulation step by step, how she'd prepared for the surgery, what precautions she'd taken for anything unexpected, and marveled at this amazing, intelligent, gifted woman he was working with, and that Delaine Harris's baby's heart was in good hands.

He'd known. In Miami and since moving to Memphis. But watching her, listening to her explanations, beat him over the head with the fact that he'd never met anyone like her.

"You aren't listening to me."

He smiled. "I've listened to every word you've said."

"You were a million miles away," she accused, her gaze narrowed.

"I was listening. There's nowhere else I'd rather be than right here with you."

Her forehead creased as she frowned. "So what were you thinking about?"

"Delaine Harris."

Natalie's brow arched. "Really?"

He leaned forward, dropped a kiss to the tip of her nose. "No worries. All my thoughts were professional."

"That's not what I— Oh, you." Natalie rolled her eyes. "I wasn't worried. Not about that."

"No worries on the surgery, either. The Harris baby is the perfect candidate. In your heart, you know that."

Her gaze met his. "I just don't want anything to go wrong. Not ever, but especially not on this first procedure."

"No matter how much you prepare, or worry, when dealing with human lives something can always go wrong."

She nodded. "I'd thought Dr. Luiz would be in surgery with me when I did this live for the first time."

"I'm sure he'd step in if you prefer?"

She shook her head. "No, I want you."

Magic words that had him grinning.

Natalie rolled her eyes again. "Again, not what I meant."

"But true," he teased, knowing his words to be so.

It wasn't a question. He didn't need her to tell him.

She'd shown him.

What was taking Matthew so long? Natalie leaned against the pillow she'd propped against the headboard. He'd disappeared while she'd been in the bathroom.

How did one get ready for bed with the great Matthew Coleman?

She'd done all her usual routine—washed her face, brushed her teeth and hair, flossed, moisturized. She'd even taken a few extra steps of freshening up all over, because she knew what the night was likely to bring.

Perhaps she should have searched for something more glamorous than the cotton pajama shorts and tank top she'd packed at her house when they'd swung by after leaving the hospital. He'd spoken with his sister and she'd asked to keep Carrie another night. But truthfully, Natalie figured no matter what she started off wearing, she'd likely end up naked before long.

She adjusted the strap of the tank, letting it fall off her shoulder, then, feeling stupid, straightened it.

"Matthew?" she called, wondering if he'd fallen asleep on the sofa or something.

"On my way," he answered, and he must really have been because he almost immediately walked into the room, bare-chested, in a pair of to-the-knee gym shorts.

He was carrying a bowl of popcorn and a large water bottle.

"What's that for?" She'd thought he'd dive straight into bed and make haste to remove her pajamas, not bring a snack.

"Us." He put the bowl and drink on the night stand. The buttery scent of popcorn filled her nostrils, making her want some even though they'd grabbed dinner on the way home from the hospital.

"We'll get popcorn in the bed," she warned, reaching out and tossing a few warm kernels in her mouth.

Not looking as if he cared if they covered the bed in popcorn, he grinned.

"Mmm, that's good." She grabbed a few more.

He picked up a remote control, pushed a button that dropped a big screen down out of the ceiling.

"Wow."

"You haven't seen anything yet," he teased, climbing into bed beside her and holding the remote out toward the screen.

"You're wrong about that."

Glancing at her, he laughed. "What's your favorite genre of movies?"

Natalie stared blankly at him.

"Come on, you have to have a favorite."

"Not really. I don't watch much television and haven't been to the movie theater in years."

"Seriously?"

Feeling self-conscious, she shrugged. "It's really not a big deal."

"Sure it is. You were in a relationship for a couple of years. Didn't he take you out?"

Touchy subject, Natalie thought. "We went for dinner."

"That's it?"

"He went with me to hospital functions. I went to his work functions. It worked for me. Obviously, it wasn't working quite so well for him."

"His law firm represents the hospital? That's why he was at Dr. Luiz's semi-retirement party?"

She nodded. "His family has a lot of connections to the hospital. It's how we met."

"I've said it before and I'll say it again: he's an idiot."

Not wanting to talk about her ex any more, she scooted closer to him and traced her fingers down the indentation in the center of his abs. "That's two of us who think so, but let's not waste time talking about him. He doesn't matter."

His skin prickled with goosebumps beneath her fingertips.

"I'm taking you to the movies, Natalie," he surprised her by saying. "You, me and Carrie. We're going next weekend."

She just stared.

"That work for you?"

Still wondering what she had gotten herself into, but knowing she was on this roller-coaster ride, Natalie nodded.

Matthew's smile was brighter than the screen he'd just clicked on when he said, "It's a date."

CHAPTER TWELVE

MOISTURE TRICKLED DOWN the back of Natalie's neck and beneath her scrubs. A surgical nurse kept the sweat from her face by dabbing gauze over it every so often. Delaine Harris's abdomen had been opened and the sweet little girl inside was being operated on while still attached by the umbilical cord. They'd been carefully making incisions into her tiny body as they threaded the smallest possible arterial catheter into her heart.

Via the catheter, Natalie and Matthew had repaired the blockage in the pulmonary artery that, once the baby was born and having to breathe on her own, would have prevented her body from getting oxygenated blood.

Everything connected with repairing the blockage had gone smoothly and they'd made the decision to repair the large ventricular defect with a patch. Using the computer for guidance and just as she'd practiced dozens of times,

Natalie placed the patch, closing the abnormal defect one painstaking suture at a time. Matthew stood on the opposite side of her, working to suture the patch as well.

As much as she wanted to glance away from the screen to meet his eyes, to see his wink of encouragement, she didn't dare look away from the image of Delaine's baby's tiny heart.

No matter. She could feel Matthew's presence, feel his encouragement as surely as if he were speaking the words.

Along with the obstetrician, a neonatologist, an anesthesiologist and a slew of nurses and surgical techs, Matthew was a valued member of the surgical team.

Having him there meant everything.

Which was a little scary.

She didn't want to get too dependent upon him. She didn't want to depend on anyone. Hadn't she learned her lesson over and over—that to depend on someone was to set oneself up for disappointment?

Natalie worked on reattaching one set of vessels while he worked on another. Considering their tiny workspace, how well they worked together was quite impressive.

Not once did he attempt to take over—he just

followed her lead, perfectly performing his repair while she made hers.

An alarm sounded, indicating that Mom's heart rate was dipping.

"Got this," the anesthesiologist assured, as he and the obstetrician made medication and fluid adjustments.

Natalie hoped they were right. Everything was proceeding according to plan, but it would be another few hours before they were done.

When they'd finally finished the baby's heart surgery and stepped back to let the obstetrician take over safely closing the baby inside her mother's uterus, Natalie felt like her insides might explode with excitement.

She'd done it.

Something she'd dreamed of doing for years, since being in residency and proposing the idea. She'd performed her first in-utero vessel transposition repair. She'd written papers on the procedure, done hundreds of computer simulations, believed it would improve the long-term outcomes of her patients.

Emotions rushed through her as she realized she'd just performed what could be the most important surgery of her career. If it worked—

it had to work—it could change the entire way "blue baby" care was approached.

Now, for the next few months, they'd wait and see if she'd been correct. Wait, and do a whole lot of praying.

Which was okay. Natalie did a lot of praying with each surgery she performed because that was someone's precious child.

Because some children were wanted and loved.

Not all kids ended up in the foster program as she had.

Just look at Carrie.

Natalie slipped off her surgical mask, slumped against the wall of the room she'd just entered, and prayed that Delaine and her baby continued to do well—better even.

"You did an amazing job, Dr. Sterling," Ben Robards, the obstetrician who'd been in on the surgery, praised when he entered the room, along with Matthew. Both removed their surgical masks. "Thanks for letting me be a part of this."

It was Ben who'd initially come to her with his patient, discussed with her the possibility of Delaine's baby being the first at Memphis

Children's to have her heart deformity repaired while still in utero.

"Without the long hours you put in, today wouldn't have been possible," she assured him. "You did a fabulous job with Delaine. The whole team did."

"Agreed," Matthew said. "Now we wait to see."

"When you think mom and baby are stable enough to consider sending home with fetal monitoring," Dr. Robards said, "I'll give you a call to be sure we cover all our bases."

"Sounds perfect."

"Nice man," Matthew commented after the obstetrician had removed his protective outer coverings from his scrubs, thoroughly cleaned his hands and left the room. "I met him briefly at Dr. Luiz's retirement party, but hadn't talked with him much until today."

Natalie still leaned against the wall and stared at him.

"Exhausted?"

"In some ways. In others, I feel exhilarated."

He grinned. "I know what you mean." First glancing through the window on the door going into the operating room to make sure no one was close to coming into the room, he reached out and cupped her face. "You were amazing in there, Dr. Sterling. Deserving of every praise Dr. Luiz ever uttered."

Casting her own nervous glance toward the doorway, Natalie smiled. "He's a smart man, that Dr. Luiz."

Matthew studied her. "Even though he played a key role in my being hired?"

Natalie hesitated only a second. "Especially because of that."

"Natalie," he groaned, leaning in to kiss her, but, wide-eyed, she pushed off the wall and shook her head.

"Uh-uh. Not at the hospital."

"Won't Carrie find it odd if I go to dinner with you unexpectedly?"

Matthew stared at the woman he'd missed in his bed the past three nights. Two nights of holding her, of waking with her next to him, and then being by himself in that big bed had just felt wrong. Not that he hadn't understood why she wanted to stay at the hospital to keep close tabs on the Harris baby.

That had been last night. Tonight, she could go home.

He'd come to her office on his way out so he

could convince her to go to dinner. Stubborn woman had refused earlier when he'd asked, just as she had the previous two evenings, and it seemed she was sticking to that trend.

"Why would she find it odd?" he asked, not understanding her line of thought. Carrie liked Natalie.

"Maybe she'd prefer to spend time with just you after being away from you all weekend."

Elaine hadn't brought Carrie home until late Sunday. Natalie had been gone for just over an hour when his sister had pulled into the drive. He hadn't wanted her to go, but from the point his sister called to say she'd be headed that way in an hour or so, Natalie had become guarded and had quickly left.

"Over spending time with us?" he clarified, trying to make sense of her reticence. "Spending time with you wouldn't bother her. She'd like it."

Natalie didn't look convinced. "Before was different because I wasn't having sex with you. It didn't matter if she didn't like me. Unless you are hoping she *doesn't* like me so you have a reason to end this now?"

She was right. What Carrie thought did matter. A lot.

"You know I don't want to end this, and Carrie already likes you," he reminded her. "Do you not want to have dinner with me, Natalie?"

"I do want to have dinner with you. It's just…"

"I have Carrie," he guessed. She wasn't saying no because of him, but because of his little girl. They'd had such a great time over the weekend, had worked together at the hospital in complete harmony. Why would she hesitate to spend time with him because of Carrie?

Looking guilty, she said, "I'm sorry. I'm just not much of a 'being around kids' person."

"You're a pediatric cardiologist," he reminded her, not bothering to hide his annoyance.

"So?" she challenged, crossing her arms over her chest as her chin lifted several notches.

"So, you make your living by spending time with kids. Carrie doesn't bite."

"I could point out that I specialize in neonatology. Most of my patients aren't even a year old." Natalie's expression didn't waver. "So don't make fun of my concerns, Matthew. This is serious."

"You think I don't know it's serious? I want to spend time with you, want you to go to dinner with me, and you won't because Carrie is going to be there." He made it sound a crime, as if she should be ashamed for saying no.

"I should stay here and work."

"Nice try, but there's nothing you have to do until bright and early in the morning."

"Have to and need to are two different things. Besides, being close in case Delaine has issues isn't a bad idea."

"You can be close without spending the night at the hospital. I live ten minutes from here," he pointed out. When she started to argue, he added, "I want to celebrate the fantastic job you did yesterday, Natalie. Away from work. This is a big deal. Let me share it with you."

For a brief second she looked as if she might relent, might go to dinner with him and Carrie, but she shook her head.

"I'm sorry to disappoint you, but I'd rather not tonight, Matthew." Her expression remained conflicted. "Please understand."

His sigh was full of frustration. "I want to talk you into changing your mind, but I'm not going to be that guy, Natalie. The one who keeps on every time he doesn't get his way. If you want to go home rather than go to dinner with me and Carrie, then you should go home."

"Thank you." A great deal of her tension visibly eased.

"But don't expect me to understand, because I don't. I really think——"

"Matthew?" she interrupted.

"Right," he said, not finishing the argument he'd been about to present. Glancing at his watch, he cursed at the time, knowing he had to get Carrie from her extended preschool program. "Am I allowed to call you once I've put her to bed?"

"I'll be here until late."

"Your boss must be a horrible slave-driver."

A smile toyed at her lips. "He's not so bad."

"Good to know." He crossed the room, wrapped his arms around her waist and pulled her in for a goodbye kiss. "I was beginning to think you didn't like him."

"I like him well enough," she admitted, staring into his eyes.

"Just well enough?" he asked, his lips hovering above hers.

"A little more." She stood on her tiptoes and kissed him.

That she initiated the kiss, that her hands wrapped around his neck and held on to him tight, just about undid every good intention Matthew had.

"No, we are not doing anything on my desk," she said, reading his mind. "You've got to pick up Carrie."

"I do."

"So go."

"I don't want to leave you."

"I'll be here tomorrow."

"Tomorrow seems like a long time from now."

Smiling, Natalie pushed him toward her office door. "Goodnight, Matthew."

"I'll call later," he promised, leaning in for a last kiss.

"I'd like that."

Matthew didn't try to talk her into dinner when Natalie said no on Thursday, but that night when he called their conversation quickly morphed into conveying his frustration.

"I want to see you outside the hospital."

"I'm on my way home now," she told him, truly being in her car driving toward her condo.

"Carrie's down for the night. What am I supposed to do? Wake her and drag her to your place so I can hold you?"

"You know I don't want you to do that."

"I miss you in my bed, Natalie."

"I miss being there," she admitted, keeping her eyes glued on the road as she drove. It had only been a few nights since she'd been there, but oh, how she missed his body pressed up against hers. How had she gone all those weeks without him?

"Come to me, Natalie." His voice was low, full of temptation.

"Now?"

"Yes."

A million responses formed in her head but none of them came out of her mouth.

"You're silent because you're rerouting your GPS to take you to my house, right?"

She couldn't go to his house. She just couldn't.

"I remember how to get to your house," she admitted. After all, she had spent most of the weekend there.

"Then you have no excuse. How soon will you be here? I'll put the popcorn on."

Natalie's cheeks heated. "No popcorn."

"You prefer something stickier?"

"I haven't eaten, but…"

"It's after nine, Natalie. You're just now leaving work and haven't had any dinner?"

She didn't deny his claim because, in her excitement over how well Delaine and her baby had been doing when she'd checked in on the pregnant woman and getting caught up in documenting her findings, Natalie had forgotten to eat.

"Your boss really is a jerk."

He sounded so outraged, she laughed. "I'll let him know you said so."

"How soon will you be here?"

"I'm not coming, Matthew. It's late. I'm going home, showering, eating, reading for a while, then going to bed."

"You can do all those things at my house."

Natalie blinked. Without even realizing it, she'd already turned onto a street that took her toward him and away from her apartment.

Natalie didn't make it home that night. Sneaking out of Matthew's bed at just before dawn to go home and grab a shower and clean clothes didn't count.

She must have had a guilty expression on her face because when she walked into the gym the next day Monica and Suzie both gave her a knowing look.

"What?"

"You saw him last night."

"I see him every day at work," she said flippantly, sliding onto the vacant elliptical next to Monica's and wondering why she was bothering working out that morning. She'd gotten more than enough exercise during the night.

"You're glowing."

"Don't be ridiculous."

"Don't bother denying that he makes you happy."

Natalie punched in her settings, then began churning away at the elliptical. All the while her mind churned with Suzie's comment.

Matthew did make her happy.

Happy in a way she didn't recall being. Which seemed a strange admission, because she hadn't been *un*happy.

Not that she'd been pleased to learn Jonathan had been cheating on her, but even then, she wouldn't have called herself unhappy. Maybe part of her had always expected him to leave.

Then along had come Matthew.

Who would also eventually leave, and then what a mess there would be in his wake.

"Are you officially dating now?"

"Our relationship is complicated," she admitted, not wanting to lie to her friends, but not wanting to dish out details either.

"Because you work together?" Monica asked.

"You like him, Nat. A lot. From the sound of things, he likes you, too," Suzie added.

Natalie nodded. Matthew did like her. It seemed unbelievable that he wanted her so much, but he did.

"I really think this guy is the one, Nat."

Natalie sighed. Her friends just didn't understand. Not really, because it wasn't them involved. No matter. She loved them anyway, as they did her. Thank goodness they'd come into her life and welcomed a lost young girl into their hearts.

Maybe, just maybe, she should thank goodness Matthew had come into her life and welcomed her into his heart, too.

If only he wouldn't eventually leave.

The popcorn wasn't as good as what Matthew had made for their in-bed movie, but Natalie wasn't complaining.

She glanced over at him. Matthew's eyes were glued on the theater's big screen playing the latest animated children's feature, but he must have sensed her gaze because he looked her way and winked.

Carrie had seemed excited to see her again, had chatted away about her school and her new friends and having gone to the zoo over the past weekend with her cousins to check up on baby giraffe Zoie's progress to making her grand entrance into the world.

Natalie felt such an affinity for the child. Probably because of the bond they shared over having both lost their parents at such a young age. Recalling the loss Carrie was dealing with made her want to wrap the girl in a hug and protect her from everything the world might throw at her.

Which was also part of why she felt the need to keep Carrie from getting too attached to her.

Natalie's gaze dropped to her hand. Her hand that was encased in a small, warm one. The girl's other hand was clasped with Matthew's. To anyone looking their way, they probably looked like a happy little family.

The reality was, her and Matthew's relationship was temporary. It was why she was so reluctant to spend time with the girl. How could she let Carrie get attached when she knew eventually she'd no longer be in her life? That she'd have to leave the child, the way so many had come in and out of her own childhood?

But the little girl taking her hand and clasping it tightly had given Natalie a warm, fuzzy feel inside, making her wish she was truly part of a family, *this* family, making her wish this were real and not temporary.

She glanced up, realized Matthew was still watching her and blushed a little that he'd caught her staring at her hand laced with Carrie's.

Could he see how torn she was? How part of her thrilled at the child's affection? How part of her wanted to shield herself and Carrie from future pain?

Although she'd not explained her feelings to him, no doubt he'd realized her current biggest hang-up centered around Carrie and not the hospital. When things went south with their relationship, work could, and likely would, be problematic. If things went sour that would prompt her to look for a department head position over her own pediatric cardiology unit. As long as things were good with Matthew, she didn't see herself stepping outside the comfortable box she currently found herself in.

Comfortable? That might be stretching it.

She wasn't comfortable with her relationship with Matthew.

Eventually, his desire for her would change. Just as Jonathan's had.

And then he'd leave.

Definitely better not to get too attached to Carrie, and not to let the innocent girl get too attached to her, when Natalie knew how that ripping away of relationships felt in the wake of tragedy.

Better for her not to get too attached to Matthew, either.

She feared she might be too late on that one.

CHAPTER THIRTEEN

NATALIE COULDN'T RECALL ever having been this nervous.

Carrie had gone to a sleepover birthday party for Matthew's youngest niece, and so he had invited Natalie over for a sleepover party at his place. She'd packed a bag and spent the night. Somehow, that morning over breakfast, he'd talked her into going with him to have a birthday lunch for his niece at his mother's. Probably because she'd caught that vulnerable look in his eyes that parental tasks to do with Carrie so often brought out in him—that look that was so at odds with everything else about him.

Still, she shouldn't have agreed.

"This is a bad idea."

Matthew glanced over at her from the driver's seat. "Why's that?"

"I shouldn't be here."

"Of course you should. I want you here."

"What about your family? What are they

going to think when I'm with you? What about your sister? She's going to know we spent the night together. Your mom, too."

"That bothers you?"

Apparently, it did.

"Don't worry. All my family will love you."

Amazingly, they seemed to do just that.

Natalie had been hugged and had her cheeks kissed a dozen times. She'd been introduced to aunts, uncles, cousins, neighbors, and hoped there wasn't a pop quiz because no way would she ever remember all their names.

Elaine shared her brother's pale blue eyes and dark hair and was a beautiful woman, as were her two daughters. Her husband was a boisterous Italian who worked in the restaurant business, but Natalie didn't catch any more details than that.

Matthew's mother was a feisty, petite woman who ran her household with a drill sergeant's efficiency yet with hugs and kisses. She had dark eyes that seemed to constantly smile. Obviously the siblings had gotten their eye color from their father, who'd passed many years before.

His mother had invited several friends and neighbors. The house was crowded, loud, warm, exactly what Natalie thought a family gathering should be. How had Matthew moved away and missed out on so much love for so many years? Nothing in Boston could have lured her away from this lovely family.

Glancing his way, she noted Matthew wore a slight scowl as he surveyed the crowded setting. Maybe he'd hoped for a small family gathering to spend quality time with his mother and sister rather than all the friends and extended family his mother had welcomed into her home. Or maybe he was worried she'd be overwhelmed by the crowd.

"You have a beautiful family, Matthew. I envy you that."

He raked his fingers through his hair, glancing around the room. "Don't envy me this."

"Your family?" she asked, confused.

"Being forced back here, giving up Boston, my life? This chaos isn't what I would have chosen."

"This?"

He gestured around the noisy room. Children ran around with parents yelling orders for them to "Be careful". And "Don't do that". Several family members cleaned the kitchen after the birthday festivities. A handful sat in the living room, watching a sports game, except for one young father who had a sleeping baby on his chest and he was catching a cat nap, as well. Others had gone out to sit on the front porch, possibly to escape some of the noise.

"I shouldn't have insisted you come here."

She was having a good time, enjoying his family and the warmth with which she'd been welcomed. Natalie arched her brow. "You don't want me here?"

"*I* don't even really want to be here." He looked around. His gaze landing on the dad with the sleeping baby on his chest. The skin pulled tight over his face, then he seemed to shake off his mood as he turned back to her. "You have to admit last night was a lot more fun."

Natalie eyed him curiously. Last night had been fun, but so was this, just in a different way. Surely he understood that? Did he feel uncomfortable around his family? Or maybe he was nervous since he knew she'd grown up without any real family life.

"I'm good and enjoying meeting your family," she assured him. "Besides, Carrie is having a great time with her cousins."

Raking his fingers through his hair, he nodded. "You're right, only…"

"Only?" she prompted.

At her frown, he tried to explain. "Don't get me wrong. I love my family. My mom and sister are the best. Just, this makes me feel…" His gaze landed on where Carrie played a board game with her cousins and some new friends, then his gaze made its way back to the dad holding his baby. "All of this makes me feel inadequate in regard to Carrie and wonder what I was thinking to ever agree to any of this. Almost to the point of claustrophobia."

Matthew knew he had revealed too much. He could see it in Natalie's surprised eyes. But watching the women, the men, interact with their kids at this party had left him daunted at the reality that he alone was responsible for Carrie. For her mental, physical and emotional well-being. If he screwed up too often, it was that innocent little girl who would pay the price.

Maybe if he'd started at the beginning preparing himself for a father role he'd be better at it, feel semi-competent. As it was, more and more he found himself wondering if Carrie would be better off living with his sister. She'd talked about the option to adopt Carrie into her own family not long after Robert and Carolyn's death, but Matthew had been reeling at the loss of his friends and hadn't been able to bear the thought of letting Carrie go. That had been self-ish of him. If he'd truly had Carrie's best interests at heart, he'd have given her to Elaine, where she'd have had a nurturing environment.

"What makes you claustrophobic makes me nostalgic for something I never had," Natalie said softly, disappointment in her eyes.

"You like this?"

She nodded. "You're lucky to have such a great family. To belong and be loved just because you were born into this family. It's something a lot of people never have."

Something *she'd* never had.

At that moment his Uncle Kenny belched, a cousin high-fived the balding man and a couple of the kids yelled out, *"Eww!"* amidst giggles.

"Yep, lucky," he mused, although none of his family's antics had ever bothered him in the past. Today felt different.

"I always got the impression you were close to your family."

"I am." He was. "Now I'm the one overthinking." He gave a low laugh, although he felt no humor. "Ignore me."

Why the day had gotten to him so completely, he wasn't sure. Just that more and more he felt inadequate in his thrust-upon role as Carrie's parent, and being here among all these other real parents made him feel like the odd man out.

"Come on, Natalie," he prompted, hoping to rid her eyes of the disillusionment. "Let's take the kids out back to play."

She looked uncertain. "Are you sure?"

Determined not to let his insecurities about Carrie put a complete damper on what had otherwise been a good day, he nodded. "Positive. Come on. Let's have some fun." The fun stuff was something he knew he could cope with, at least.

His mother's back yard was a fenced-in area that was approximately two hundred by two hundred feet. A sandbox and a swing set were off to the left corner.

"Swings or sand?"

Natalie's eyes widened. "Aren't we just watching the kids?"

"What's the fun in that?" He took her hand and walked her over to the swing set. "Have a seat, Natalie."

"I…"

"Are you afraid of heights or get motion sickness?"

She shook her head.

"Then sit."

She sat.

Expecting him to take the swing next to hers, she'd barely gotten her grip when he warned, "Hold on tight." Then gave her a hefty push.

Natalie had been on a swing before. At some point during her childhood, she was sure she had. Probably during grammar school. But she had no recall of having had someone push her. She smiled.

"Me, too!" Carrie pleaded as she climbed up on the swing next to Natalie's. "Push me, too!"

Matthew immediately gave the child a big push, setting her swing in motion and triggering a trail of pleased squeals.

Matthew's eldest niece joined in, adding her pleas to be pushed.

The moment his niece was settled in the next swing Matthew added her to his routine, giving her a couple of pushes to get her moving, too. He moved back and forth between the three swings, keeping them all going higher and higher. Carrie was squealing with delight, as was Liz.

Way back in the recesses of her mind, a memory tugged at Natalie. Or maybe more of an emotion than memory. One that had a lot to do with being tossed from one foster home to another. To never having *had* anyone like Matthew to push her on a swing.

"Higher, Uncle Matthew! Higher!" Carrie cried.

Carrie had lost both of her parents, had no other family, just as Natalie hadn't. She could easily have ended up in the same situation as Natalie had.

"To the moon and back?" he asked, getting a resounding "Yes!" as his answer.

Thank goodness she had Matthew.

He thought he was inadequate in his parent-figure role. From time to time those insecurities bled forth, such as today. Natalie wished he could see what she saw when she watched him with Carrie, when he spoke of the child, the love that shone in his eyes.

Natalie smiled at the happiness of the moment.

"Me, too, Uncle Matthew. Me, too," Liz cried.

If Natalie had thought Matthew was going to let her swing slow as he kept the other two girls going, she'd been wrong. He gave a hard push any time her swing appeared to be slowing. His youngest niece climbed to the top of the slide for a bird's-eye view and cheered them onward.

"Do you want my swing?" Natalie called to the girl.

The just-turned-four birthday girl shook her head.

"If you decide you do, let me know," she offered.

Giggles abounded from Matthew's other two swingers. He seemed to have relaxed and let out a few laughs. The happy sounds made Natalie warm inside.

This, she thought. This was what she wanted.

The crazy, loud chaos from indoors. The preciousness of this moment with Matthew and the kids. Only she wanted it to be real. For her and Matthew to be a couple, for Carrie to be theirs.

She wanted a family. Matthew's family.

Which scared her.

To want those things was foolish and a waste of energy. Maybe someday she'd have this, a family of her own, but it wouldn't be with Matthew. He'd made that plain in Florida and again in Memphis. He wasn't looking for anything long-term, wasn't that what he'd said?

She closed her eyes, gave in to the rhythm of the moving swing, pushing off each time her feet came near the ground, welcoming the momentum each time Matthew's hands made contact and gave a hardy push.

Higher and higher she went, her mind clearing and a sense of flying taking hold, making her want to stretch her arms out and go soaring through the air.

Lightness came over her and before she thought better of it she leapt out of the swing, laughing as she landed on her feet with her arms outstretched. "Ta-da!"

"What was that?" Matthew laughed from where he stood behind the swings, giving the girls another push.

"Me reliving my youth," she blurted out, although it wasn't exactly true. She couldn't recall having ever jumped out of a swing in the past, just had memories of watching other kids do so while playing with each other as she watched from the sidelines.

"Looks good on you."

Her eyes met his. Her breath hiccupped in her throat. No wonder she wanted this. Wanted him. Despite his struggles over his thrust-upon parenting role, he was a good man, was an excellent heart surgeon, was a fantabulous lover and was beautiful to look upon, inside and out.

"Thank you," she told him as she made her

way back over to her swing and set it in motion again, aided by the feel of Matthew's hands against her bottom for a brief moment.

She definitely should have played more on swings as a child. And more taking chances in her life after that, instead of always playing it safe.

Or was this her brain's way of trying to convince her that taking a chance with Matthew was okay? That she wasn't making the biggest mistake of her life by being here with him today? That she wasn't setting herself up for horrific pain? That she wasn't setting sweet little Carrie up for pain, too?

Leaning back into the swing, Natalie closed her eyes and gave in to the swinging motion again.

"I want to jump, too," Carrie called out.

"Go for it," he encouraged. "You got this."

Natalie opened her eyes just in time to see Carrie let go of the swing's chains and do exactly what Natalie had done minutes before.

Only Carrie's flight wasn't a liberating soar. Instead, she flailed through the air.

"Carrie! No!" Natalie warned, planting her feet on the ground to slow her swing the moment the child let go and practically flipped out of the swing seat.

She reached Carrie milliseconds after the little girl hit the ground.

Carrie's leap from her swing and into the air played in slow motion in Matthew's head. Even before she hit the ground, he knew her landing wasn't going to be pretty. She'd come off the swing too high and at the wrong angle, almost as if she had just let go and fallen forward out of the swing rather than leaping.

If only the jump really had been in slow motion and he could have gotten to her in time to catch her.

If only he could move at all.

Carrie's returning swing slapped against his chest in his frozen state as she landed on the ground hard, and all wrong.

"Carrie!" Natalie knelt next to the unmoving child.

Fear slammed Matthew, paralyzing him. Fear that he'd let something happen to Robert's child. Fear that she might be seriously hurt. Fear that he'd failed so quickly, so *horribly* at this parenting thing.

His heart wrenched as Carrie's cries filled

the air, but so did a sense of relief. Cries required life.

He'd had horrors of her landing on her neck.

As Natalie knelt beside her she sat up, tears streaming down her face and sobs escaping from her lips.

Seeing her moving had Matthew wanting to sob, too.

He should go to her. It was what a parent would do. He should take her in his arms and comfort her.

It was what *Natalie* was doing.

"What hurts, sweetie?" she asked quickly, her gaze raking over Carrie, searching for injury, connecting with how Carrie held her left arm at an awkward angle.

Eyes wide, she gasped between tears, "My arm."

Carrie was hurt and he was frozen in place like a blazing idiot.

"Try to hold still, sweetie," Natalie encouraged. "I'm going to check you over."

But Carrie was panicking, guarding against Natalie's attempts to do so. Other than scraped knees Matthew didn't recall any injury in the child's short four years with her parents, so the fall had to have her frightened.

Why wasn't he moving toward her? Why wasn't he checking her? What was wrong with him? He should be the one checking Carrie. She was his *responsibility.*

"Am I going to die like Daddy and Momma?" she sobbed, her big brown eyes glassy from her tears.

Failure sucker-punched Matthew in the gut. He hadn't even considered that she might associate her pain to her parents' death.

Natalie kissed Carrie's forehead. "No, sweetie, of course not. But you are hurt and I need to check you."

She gently examined Carrie's arm. It didn't take a degree to see the odd angle of her forearm. Matthew's stomach threatened to spill the birthday cake he'd eaten earlier. How could he have let this happen?

"Is Carrie okay, Uncle Matthew?" Liz asked, tugging on his shirt and drawing Natalie's gaze to him momentarily.

Her expression was one of confusion—as in, why wasn't he by her side helping check Carrie, helping reassure her that she was going to be okay?

Good question, with the only answer being that he was a total failure of a parent.

His other niece squatted down next to Carrie. Mandy patted her right shoulder, telling her it was going to be okay.

"She's hurt, Uncle Matthew," Liz said, sounding a little panicked. "Carrie is hurt."

He glanced down at the little girl staring up at him with big eyes that begged him to do something.

Do something, he ordered himself. He was a renowned heart surgeon, had never frozen like this no matter what the circumstances. What was wrong with him?

"Matthew?" Natalie's voice broke into his self-recriminations.

Snapping out of his frozen state, he scooped Liz into his arms and moved toward what was difficult for him to look at because Carrie's broken limb was the culmination of all he was lacking as a parent.

"She will be okay." He wasn't sure if he was talking to himself or to his niece. "But we're going to have to get her to the emergency room to get a special picture taken of her arm."

He looked directly at Carrie, hating that the child was having to deal with anything negative so soon on the heels of losing her parents.

"You've broken your arm," Natalie told her in

a calm voice. Much calmer than Matthew felt. "You're going to need the bone reset, okay? We're going to have to take you to the hospital," she continued.

Hopefully, that was all Carrie would need done. She looked so tiny, so helpless sitting there crying, tears staining her shirt, so much of his two best friends blended in her features.

How could he have allowed anything to happen to her?

"I don't want to go to the hospital," Carrie cried, looking at Matthew as if he were responsible and clinging to Natalie as if she was a lifeline.

He didn't blame her. If he'd known what he was doing, he wouldn't have allowed this to happen.

"Can we come?" both nieces asked in unison.

Setting Liz down, Matthew knelt beside Carrie. "Go in with the girls and tell the others what happened," he told Natalie. "I'm going to load Carrie into the car. Meet me around front."

"I want Natalie!" Carrie cried, clenching her fingers into Natalie's shirt. "Please don't leave me."

"And could you grab a clean button-up shirt and shorts from one of the girls for Carrie to put on when we're through at the hospital?" Matthew continued, ignoring Carrie's pleas.

Natalie looked hesitant, but then pried Carrie's hands free of her shirt, took Liz's and Mandy's hands into hers and headed into the house with the girls in tow.

Taking care not to bump Carrie's left arm, Matthew scooped her into his arms and stood with her.

She felt so little in his arms, so helpless. Shame that he'd let this happen to her filled him. Shame that he hadn't done better by her. He'd known he wasn't cut out for parenthood yet he'd played around at it for the past five months, pretending he could do this.

Obviously he couldn't, and needed to do what was right for Carrie.

Natalie and Matthew's family rushed out of the house, requested items in hand, just as Matthew was buckling Carrie into her car seat. He shut her door and motioned for Natalie to get in the driver's seat.

"Could you drive so I can sit back here with her? I didn't want to put her into her car seat, but two wrongs don't equal a right and it's my job to keep her safe."

His tone implied that he thought the little girl's fall was his fault.

Natalie reached out to touch him, to reassure him that Carrie's injuries were an accident, but he shrugged away her touch.

"Oh, honey." Matthew's mother winced, taking a peep into the car at the child. "Grandma will be there with you in a few."

"It's okay, Mom," Matthew immediately corrected. "Stay here with your company. I'll call when I know something."

His sister and a few of the other guests said things, too, but they blurred in Natalie's head. Everything was blurring in her head.

Why had Matthew shrugged away her touch? For that matter, why had he stood at the swing for so long after Carrie's fall?

Wanting to ask him about his odd behavior, but knowing now wasn't the time, Natalie climbed in, pushed the button to start the car and had them on their way.

Her mind racing, she drove on autopilot.

Carrie went back and forth between whimpering and crying on the drive to the hospital, saying she didn't want to go to the emergency room, that she didn't want Matthew, that she wanted her mommy and daddy.

As she glanced in the rear-view mirror Matthew's pale, gaunt expression tore at Natalie.

"You're going to be okay, Carrie," he soothed from the back seat. "This is going to be okay."

He didn't address her request for her parents, but then, what could he say?

The emergency room doctor consulted a pediatric orthopedic surgeon who'd taken Carrie to surgery to reset the bones, leaving Natalie and Matthew in the waiting room.

Carrie was wheeled away while Matthew looked as if he might pull rank and stay at her side during surgery.

Natalie understood. Part of her wanted to be at the child's side to make sure nothing went wrong, too. Logically, she knew that Matthew or herself would just be in the way, a distraction that might cause a problem. They needed to let the surgeon do what he'd been trained to do.

She tried to comfort Matthew, but again, he wasn't receptive to her touch. Natalie sank into one of the waiting room chairs and watched him pace back and forth.

His mother, sister and a slew of other family members arrived minutes behind them, despite Matthew's request that they stay home. His family hugged him and comforted him and he semi-let them. Natalie watched, feeling more and more like an outsider.

They'd been waiting for what seemed like hours before Matthew got a call Carrie was in Recovery, that everything had gone fine and they'd allow him to come to see her very soon.

"I can't believe I let this happen," he berated himself, pacing across the lobby while he waited on the okay to head to the recovery room.

"These things happen." Matthew's mother wrapped him in a hug again and plopped several big kisses on his cheeks. "Don't you recall how many broken bones you and Robert had between the two of you? His mother and I knew the emergency staff by name."

"That was different."

"How?"

"We were boys, and Carrie has already suffered so much."

"Being boys makes it okay how?" his sister piped up. "Just because you and Robert were guys didn't make it okay. You scared us all several times. Remember that time you…?"

While his family continued to go on and on about the past, about how accidents happened and how a parent couldn't bubble-wrap their child, more and more unease took hold inside Natalie.

Matthew hadn't wanted her touch, her comfort.

Of course he hadn't. She was nothing more than a temporary lover.

As she recalled her thoughts when they'd been playing on the swings, her longings for their relationship to be real, nausea churned.

She was getting too involved in his life, in Carrie's.

Seeing the child hurt had torn at her heart, had filled her with a protectiveness for the girl that surprised her. She'd have willingly taken Carrie's place, taken the pain so she wouldn't have to experience it.

Natalie wasn't supposed to get attached, nor was she supposed to let the child get attached to her.

Carrie's pleas for her to stay echoed through her mind, reminding her of her own silent cries over the years not to be left behind yet again by one foster parent after another.

Yet she'd always been left.

Just as she'd be left behind this time, too, if she didn't make a preemptive move.

Matthew's mother had her arm wrapped

around him and was telling another childhood story. Part of Natalie would have liked to hear it—and all of her would have liked to know what it felt like to have a mother's arm wrapped around her. It had been so long since she'd been held with love. None of her foster parents had really shown her love. The McCulloughs had been wonderful, encouraging, but they'd not been warm and fuzzy kind of people. Jonathan sure hadn't loved her. Matthew's touch gave a glimpse of what it could be like, but she didn't want to fool herself. He didn't love her.

She needed to get away, to escape childhood memories and personal demons, to go somewhere to decompress, to get her head on straight and put an end to this fiasco she was caught up in with Matthew.

It was time to leave.

CHAPTER FOURTEEN

"WHERE DID YOU GO? Do you have any idea how embarrassed I was when I came back from seeing Carrie, expecting you to be waiting, and my family said they hadn't seen you since prior to my going to Recovery?" Matthew demanded, storming into Natalie's office and closing the door behind him with a loud thud.

Looking up from her desk, Natalie cringed, but didn't defend her actions. Then again, what could she say? She'd bailed when he'd needed her, when Carrie had been hurt.

How could she have just left without a word?

At first, he'd thought she'd slipped out to go to the restroom. When he'd finally gotten to see Carrie in Recovery and had reassured himself she was going to be okay despite his poor care, Natalie was nowhere to be found.

He waited for her to say something, pacing across her office, then turning toward her. "Why?"

She didn't quite meet his eyes. "I didn't belong."

"I invited you. Of course you belonged. Probably more so than I did."

Visibly rattled, she shook her head. "I was just a temporary lover, Matthew. Taking me to your family function was inappropriate."

"A temporary lover?" He frowned. "We're dating, Natalie."

"We were," she said quietly.

He stared at her. "We could have had something really great while it lasted."

"You think that's fair to Carrie? To bring someone into her life, let her get close to them, and then when you get bored and say adios, then what? You think Carrie isn't going to suffer?" She stood, leaned toward him. "I assure you, Carrie will be hurt by the women you have come and go in your life."

"What women I have come and go? There's only been you for months, Natalie. There are no other women."

She looked taken aback at his admission. What had she thought? That he'd been dating woman after woman since Miami, before moving to Memphis?

"But you're probably right. That's just one

more in a long line of things I'll do wrong where Carrie is concerned."

He'd always thought of himself as a great uncle. Being Carrie's uncle had been fun. He could sweep in, have a good time with her without any responsibilities. But he had never been meant to be her father. That had been Robert's place.

Only Robert wasn't here, and Matthew was doing a crappy job of trying to fill his friend's shoes.

He'd liked his life. He had liked being a bachelor, being devoted to his career, being a best friend, being an uncle. He wasn't sure he liked anything about his current situation—especially his failing relationship with the woman across from him.

"Our ending whatever this is between us now, before anyone gets hurt, is for the best."

Matthew narrowed his gaze. "The best for whom?"

"Everyone."

Ending things with Natalie didn't feel like the best thing. But maybe she was right and he needed to think of Carrie, of doing what was best for her.

Which didn't include being raised by someone who had no clue what he was doing.

Two weeks had passed since Carrie's accident. Two weeks in which Natalie had avoided Matthew as much as possible, as she was doing now by hiding out in her office working on charts.

She'd assisted during two surgeries with him, but had otherwise not spent more than a few awkward minutes with him here and there when their paths crossed in the neonatal unit or in the cardiac lab.

Her heart ached with missing him, but it was better things had ended sooner rather than later. The longer their dalliance had gone on the more difficult their demise would have been. The harder on Carrie.

The harder on Natalie.

She didn't think she could handle much more than her current devastation. She missed him so much. Missed Carrie so much, too. Not that she was admitting it to anyone. Not to Monica, Suzie or Dr. Luiz, who'd stopped by to question her about what had happened between her and Matthew.

Nothing. Nothing had happened.

Nothing ever would happen.

The University of Florida had contacted her about a research opportunity for a new surgical device they hoped to bring to the market and needed someone to head up the project. They'd requested she come for an interview.

An interview she was considering.

She wouldn't have to see Matthew anymore. Wouldn't have to think of him anymore. Would be able to forget he'd ever existed.

Nor would she have to wonder about Carrie. Wonder how the little girl was healing, how she was coping with having her arm in a sling.

She didn't want to think about Matthew, or Carrie.

She'd go to the interview. What would it hurt to find out more?

"Have you seen Carrie?"

At Matthew's barging into her office, Natalie jumped, startled at his interruption and frantic appearance. "What? No, why would I have seen her?"

The hopeful expression on his face fell, replaced by one of pure wreckage. "She's gone. She was in the yard at preschool, there one minute and gone the next. Video surveillance shows her on a computer, then sneaking out. They've already got the police out looking for her."

Panic filled Natalie. The girl was only four. So many things could have happened.

He glanced around her office as if still hoping to spot the child. "I think she overheard me talking to Elaine about arranging for her to go and live with them."

Shock reverberated through Natalie. "What? Why would you do that?"

"Because I thought she'd be better off without me." He sighed, raked his fingers through his hair, turning quickly to leave. "If you hear from her, call me."

Standing, Natalie nodded. "Can I help look for her?"

He paused, his shoulders sagging, and nodded. "There are officers on their way to talk to me, get photos of her, et cetera." His pale eyes lifted, full of pain. "Liz told Elaine that Carrie had been talking about taking a trip. I think she's run away because she thinks I don't want her anymore." His voice broke, then he sucked in a deep breath. "The police are checking the airport and bus stations in case she made it that far." His eyes bereft blue pools, he met her gaze. "What am I going to do if I don't find her?"

Despite everything wrong between them, Natalie couldn't help herself. She walked to the other side of her desk and wrapped her arms around him tight. "I'm so sorry, Matthew. I know they'll find her soon and you can tell her how much you love and need her."

He nodded, then seemed to realize he was standing still instead of looking for Carrie, and extricated himself from her hold. "I'd better go. The police are coming to the house."

Natalie would have offered to go with him, but he left her office as quickly as he'd burst into it.

Carrie was gone. She had possibly run away. Had possibly overheard Matthew talking to his sister about letting Carrie live with her family. Had she felt the same abandonment Natalie had when she'd been shuffled from one foster home to another?

Walking around to her desk, Natalie closed out her computer program. Her brain was shot. She wasn't going to accomplish anything until Carrie was found. The sheer terror she felt at the thought of the girl being on her own couldn't begin to compare to what Matthew must be feeling.

Especially as he was blaming himself.

She wanted to be with him. To comfort him. To help him look for Carrie. But she had no right. He'd only come to her, asked if she'd seen the child because he'd been desperate and had thought Carrie might have reached out to her. If only.

Natalie pulled her phone from her scrubs pocket and checked it, hoping it would magically ring and Carrie be on the other end. Nothing happened, of course.

Restless, she flipped through her messages. One in particular caught her eye.

An alert from Memphis Zoo.

Heart pounding, Natalie grabbed her keys and purse.

Natalie searched the crowd in front of the giraffe exhibit at the zoo. Not an easy feat as the pending birth of Zoie had captured more than just Carrie's heart and people were everywhere, waiting to catch their first glimpse of the giraffe. The weather was just windy enough to have folks bundled up in light jackets and hats.

Please be here, Natalie prayed. *Please. Please. Please.*

Continuing to make her way through the big-screen spectators, Natalie was just about to decide she'd been ridiculous to think she'd known where the girl was when a familiar voice called out.

"Natalie! I knew you'd come!" Carrie beamed, jumping up and down in her excitement. "Isn't it wonderful?"

Finding her was the most wonderful thing ever.

Natalie collapsed to her knees and pulled the girl into her arms, being careful not to jar Carrie's left arm, safely tucked into its sling.

"Carrie," she breathed against the child's head. "Never run off like that again! Thank God you're okay."

When she pulled back, the girl was eyeing her curiously and giggled. "I'm not the one having a baby giraffe."

If not for the seriousness of the moment, Natalie would have smiled at the child's logic. "Everyone is looking for you. We were scared something had happened. Your Uncle Matthew is beside himself."

A sheepish look came over Carrie's face. "I'm in trouble, aren't I?"

Still not quite believing she'd found her, Natalie nodded. "You really scared him, your family, me," she added, pulling her phone out to call

Matthew. "You shouldn't have left without telling anyone where you were going."

"But I wanted to see Zoie be born and I was going to go back to school before time to be picked up!"

Natalie's heart pounded as Matthew picked up on the first ring.

"I'm with Carrie," she rushed out, wanting to ease his worry as quickly as possible. "We're at the zoo."

Matthew's breath whooshed out over the phone. "The zoo? She's okay?"

"She's fine. I found her at the giraffe exhibit. They have a big screen set up as Zoie is about to be born. She wanted to be here."

"Thank God." He disconnected the call to notify his family that he'd found Carrie.

"Is he mad?"

Staring at the child, Natalie nodded. "You gave him a bad fright. He loves you very, very much."

Carrie nodded, then looked uncertain. "I make his life," she paused, sounding out the word, "complicated."

Which must be part of what she'd overheard with his conversation with his sister.

"Don't worry about that now, okay? Your

Uncle Matthew would do anything for you, Carrie. He wants you to have the very best in life." Carrie nodded as if she understood what Natalie was saying, but Natalie wasn't sure the child did, or even could at her young age. "Why didn't you just wait and ask him bring you to the zoo after preschool?"

"It might have been too late. I might have missed Zoie being born!"

Unsure what to say, Natalie hugged the little girl, then sat down on the pavement next to her to watch the screen along with the dozens of others who were there. When Carrie scooted next to her, Natalie automatically pulled her into her lap and wrapped her arms around her. Carrie laced their fingers and leaned back against her as if it was the most natural thing in the world.

This, Natalie found herself thinking again. She wanted this.

Was that why she'd run from the hospital? Because of how much she wanted Matthew and Carrie as her own? Because of how it had hit her, scared her?

On the big screen, they watched as little Zoie came into the world, and cheers sounded from all around. Natalie and Carrie cheered right along with the others.

Carrie cocked her head, grinning up at Natalie with a look of pure awe. "That was amazing."

It was.

Sharing the moment with Carrie had been amazing, too.

She might have said more, but her phone rang.

"Where are you? I can't spot you in this crowd."

Helping Carrie to her feet first, Natalie stood, spotted Matthew and waved.

"There. I see you."

He disconnected the call.

Carrie's hand slipped into hers. "I don't want to leave until Zoie takes her first step! Make Uncle Matthew promise!"

"I'm not sure I can stop him."

Carrie looked up at her with big, trusting eyes. "Just ask him to stay and he will. He'd do anything for you."

Natalie wasn't so sure.

"Carrie." Matthew scooped the child into his arms, hugged her close, kissed the top of her head. "I have never been so scared in my whole life."

"Sorry," came the muffled reply.

He set her down, knelt to her level. "What you did isn't okay, but we'll talk about it when we get home." Holding on to Carrie's hand, he stood. "Thank you so much for finding her, Natalie."

Carrie gave Natalie a pleading look.

"You're welcome. Can Carrie watch with me a few more minutes?" At Matthew's look of complete confusion, Natalie added, "Please. It would mean a lot if Carrie could watch Zoie's first steps with me."

"Please, Uncle Matthew?" Carrie said, giving him a big-eyed look. "It would mean a lot to me, too."

He glanced down at the girl, tugged at the hair that poked out from beneath her cap. "I'm not sure you get a say at the moment. I still can't believe you did this. You're not going to be playing with that tablet computer for a long time."

Carrie hesitated at that, then cranked up the volume of her big brown eyes. Matthew sighed.

"But, since we're here, it would be a shame to miss Zoie's first steps."

After Matthew had reassured his family that Carrie was okay yet again, bathed the child and put her to bed, he turned to the woman who'd been with him all evening. He'd expected Natalie to leave right after his arrival at the zoo, but she hadn't.

Probably because smart little Carrie had used her as a shield from how upset he was at what she'd done. They'd had a long talk and the child had promised never to pull a similar stunt again.

"I've been meaning to ask—how *did* you know she'd be at the zoo?" he asked when he went back into his living room.

Natalie shrugged. "After you left my office, I pulled my phone out and saw the alert that Zoie was about to be born."

"Thank God you did. Anything could have happened to her."

"You have to admit, what she did was quite impressive for a child that's not quite five. You're going to have your hands full when she hits her teenaged years." Natalie averted her gaze, then asked a question so soft he barely heard. "I heard you talking to her in her room. Did you mean what you told her?"

"About how foolish I was to think I could ever let her go live with anyone other than myself?"

Natalie nodded.

"Every word. She's mine. For better or worse,

she's stuck with me for the rest of her life. I was a fool to think I could let her go, that she'd be better off elsewhere."

"Good. She loves you. Not that that doesn't mean she's not going to give you a run for your money at times."

"That she will," he agreed, sinking onto the sofa next to her. "You going to help me keep her in line when she does?"

A look of guilt passed over her face. "Who knows where either of us will be when Carrie's older?"

Then he knew. Natalie planned to leave Memphis.

A new wave of panic swept over him. Different from the one that had hit him when he'd learned Carrie was missing, but one that ripped at his insides all the same.

"When?"

"When what?"

"When are you leaving?"

"I'm sorry." She went to stand. "I didn't mean to stay beyond my welcome."

He grabbed her wrist, pulled her back down beside him. "That isn't what I mean and you know it."

"I can't give you an answer on where I'll be in ten years."

"Or even in six months?"

Another flash of guilt contorted her face. "I'd rather not discuss it."

"Because you're leaving Memphis Children's?"

"I didn't say that."

"You didn't say you weren't."

She dropped her head back against the sofa, closed her eyes. "It would be better for both of us if I left."

Matthew was suddenly struck by the memory that Robert had always said someday he'd meet someone and know exactly how Robert had felt about Carolyn. Matthew hadn't really believed his friend. What Robert and Carolyn had had wasn't what most people had. It wasn't what anyone else Matthew had ever known had had. They'd been best friends and colleagues as well as lovers.

He finally understood what his friend had been telling him.

Understood and wanted all it had to offer.

He took her hand into his. "I want you, Natalie. In my life. In Carrie's life, helping me with her. Because I'm falling for you."

CHAPTER FIFTEEN

NATALIE WAS SURE she'd misheard. Matthew couldn't have just said he was falling for her. Why would he say that? Why now?

But she knew. The scare with Carrie had him overly emotional tonight.

"I think you're just grateful I helped you find Carrie and that's why you think you want me."

He laughed. "You think how I feel toward you is gratitude?"

"That and that your friends died and you have a void in your life, Matthew. A void you're trying to fill and I just happened to come along at the right time."

"Robert dying gutted me. He was my best friend from my earliest memories. But you and I have nothing to do with any of that." He stood, paced across his living room. "But if that's what your thoughts are when I tell you I'm falling for you, then I guess that says everything, doesn't it?"

"I suppose so." She stood, knowing it was past time she left. She should have gone long ago. Or not have given in to Carrie's request that she come home with them in the first place.

She might not have, except she'd been so worried about the girl, felt so connected to her, and wanted to make sure Matthew reassured her that he wasn't ever going to leave her.

He wasn't. Natalie knew that in her heart. Carrie would always be loved and cared for.

"Thanks for coming, Dr. Sterling. I'd thought you'd want to be here."

"You thought right." At the call from Dr. Robards, Natalie had dropped what she was doing and scrubbed in for surgery. Cesarean sections weren't her thing, but she did want to be there for this particular one.

"I wish we'd had longer before Delaine went into labor."

"Me too, but I couldn't get the labor stopped and can't delay any longer without worrying the baby is going to get into distress."

"A month is a blessing," Natalie assured, following him into the surgical suite where Delaine's baby would soon be born. "I just hoped for longer healing time prior to birth."

"As did we all."

Natalie glanced at Matthew. She should have known that Dr. Robards would have called him, too. Actually, the room was filled with neonatologists and specialists, all ready to jump into action when Delaine's baby entered the world.

Natalie avoided meeting Matthew's gaze. What was the point?

They'd said what needed to be said.

Two weeks had passed since Carrie's zoo trip. Two weeks in which Natalie had missed Matthew and the little girl, but knew she was doing the right thing in staying away.

She'd flown to Florida the previous Friday, met with the execs who had the power to extend the generous package she'd been offered. It was a wonderful opportunity, but she'd yet to make her final commitment.

"Witnessed many births?" Dr. Robards asked.

Natalie wasn't sure whether he spoke to Matthew or to her, but Matthew was who answered.

"I delivered a few babies during med school, but the only one I've been in on for the past ten years is my goddaughter's."

Dr. Robards made a cut along Delaine's bikini line close to where she'd been cut for last month's surgery on the baby's heart. "Nothing like witnessing the miracle of life. Been in on thousands, but each one never fails to humble me."

Within seconds, he was pulling Delaine's baby from her womb, handing her over to the nurse, who brought her to the waiting incubator and neonatologist.

The neonatologist worked rapidly on the premature baby, doing a quick assessment, clearing the airway and inserting a breathing tube.

While monitors and lines were attached, Natalie and Matthew performed an ultrasound on the baby's tiny heart.

"We have good flow," Natalie said, relief filling her. Delaine's baby was early, but, at thirty weeks, had a fighting chance. "Just look. Her little heart is working."

Matthew tried not to let Natalie's joy get to him, but was happy with what he was seeing, too. The baby's chest, although scarred, looked great for a month out from surgery. As they'd predicted, healing had been accelerated in utero.

"She's not out of the woods yet, but, I admit, what I'm seeing is encouraging."

Natalie nodded, stepping back so the neonatologist could check a line.

At this point, taking care of the baby's prematurity needs took precedence over her heart surgery, which thus far seemed a success. Hopefully, nothing would happen to change that status.

Natalie and Matthew left the unit together, stripped out of their surgical gear and trashed the protective equipment.

"Carrie okay?"

Surprised by Natalie's question, he paused. "She's good. We've started counseling to help us, mostly me, deal with our grief and our new family dynamics."

"That's good. Carrie is so resilient. She's going to be fine."

"Resilient and brilliant."

Natalie nodded. "Have you taken her back to see Zoie?"

"We've practically taken up residence at the zoo."

Recalling her own zoo adventure with the girl as they'd watched Zoie's birth, Natalie smiled. "I'm sure that makes her happy."

Matthew wanted to ask what made Natalie happy, but what was the point? Obviously, he wasn't the answer.

* * *

"You want to talk about this?"

Natalie glanced up to see her former boss standing in her office doorway, her resignation letter in hand, then glanced back at her computer screen to save the work she'd been charting. She motioned for him to come into her office.

"There's really not anything to say. It's a great opportunity."

"That's not why you typed this letter," Dr. Luiz corrected, causing Natalie to look up from where she'd been studying her computer screen to keep from having to meet his gaze.

"If you're talking about Dr. Coleman, I accepted the fact that he was given the position I'd hoped I'd fill weeks ago."

The man she'd admired above all others stared at her so intently she could avoid his gaze no longer. Still, she owed him nothing beyond that she'd given him a copy of her resignation first. She had two others ready to be delivered—one to the board and one to Matthew.

Dr. Luiz walked over, sat down in the chair opposite Natalie's desk, and regarded her for long, silent moments. "From the time I met you as a bright-eyed resident, I've felt a special bond with you, Natalie. Treated you almost as if you were my daughter. I want good things for you."

Feeling a wave of emotion wash over her, Natalie waited for him to continue. He didn't disappoint.

"When I first announced my intent to semi-retire, I never questioned that you could step up to fill the vacancy. I've no doubt you'd have done so successfully if the circumstances were different, because you'd have put your whole heart, your whole being into this hospital."

He was right. She would have.

"If relocating is what you believe in your heart is right for you, then I support your decision."

Natalie closed her eyes. Accepting the offer was the right decision.

"But I don't agree that it is in your best interests to relocate. I want more for you than that, but I'm not convinced you want more for yourself."

She arched her brow.

"Something changed for you in Miami. I couldn't put my finger on it until I saw you with Matthew. Hiring him was the right thing for Memphis Children's, but it was also the right thing for you."

"You're wrong." It would have been better if Matthew had stayed a fantasy fling.

Wouldn't it?

Dr Luiz leaned forward. "I don't know everything that happened between you two, but I do know you need to figure it out before anyone else sees this."

He crumpled up her resignation letter and tossed it onto her desk.

His words making her question conclusions she'd already come to, she shook her head. "There are a lot of things you don't know. Just take my word for it when I say that taking this job is the right thing."

"Lucky for them that you think so. Pity for you."

Dr. Luiz was wrong. The position in Florida opened a whole new world of opportunities. She'd be a fool to stay. Staying meant seeing Matthew regularly. She needed to forget him. To forget the things he made her long for.

Natalie winced. She wasn't longing for anything.

She wasn't.

If she was, she'd have reacted differently when Matthew had confessed he was falling for her, right?

She wouldn't have questioned his motives in what he'd said. Wouldn't have assumed that he was only saying he wanted her because she'd found Carrie and he'd been overcome with emotion.

At his words, she'd locked up inside, felt panicked. She'd felt the need to run, been scared to believe him.

Most of the people who'd come into her life had been temporary, had come and gone, and she was the one left behind.

Why should she expect him to be any different?

Emotions were messy, set a person up to get hurt. She'd been hurt enough during her lifetime. More than enough.

She hurt now.

Shocked by her admission, Natalie dropped her head onto her desk, the wadded-up letter crunching beneath her forehead.

Ugh. What was she doing?

Leaving for Florida. Was that nothing more than running away because she was afraid of Matthew, of what he made her want? Afraid of caring for Carrie?

Afraid or not, she did care. And she did want.

Straightening, Natalie sucked in a deep breath,

fought back the moisture accumulating in her eyes, and rubbed her temples.

She'd pushed Matthew away, had shut him out, because she'd been afraid of his leaving her someday.

Only, what if he didn't ever leave? What if he could love her, really love her, and she could be a real part of their family?

Matthew wasn't nearly as enthralled with Zoie as Carrie, but the baby giraffe was growing on him. Which was just as well, since Carrie would have them visiting daily if he'd agree.

Fortunately, some days she was satisfied with online viewing via the Zoie cam—but not today.

"Uncle Matthew, can we get ice cream when we finish visiting Zoie?" Liz asked, tugging on his hand. "Momma says we can if you're okay with it."

Matthew shot his sister a *Gee, thanks* look, then grinned at his niece. "Sure thing, kiddo. If the three of you are good, then ice cream it is. Two scoops, even."

"We're always good," Mandy pointed out matter-of-factly.

Matthew laughed. "Most of the time."

"Natalie?" Carrie's surprised question had

Matthew turning toward where the child was looking.

Sure enough, Natalie stood a few feet from them, holding a stuffed giraffe and looking uncertain about whether to approach.

"I've missed you." Carrie had no qualms in running over and wrapping her good arm around Natalie. "Did you see Zoie? Isn't she just the cutest?"

Natalie lowered her gaze to look at Carrie. "She is, and I've missed you, too. I bought this for you." She held out the stuffed giraffe. "I thought you might like to hold her when you're watching Zoie on your computer tablet—if you're allowed to use it now," she added with a smile.

"Thank you. I love her." Carrie took the gift and gave the giraffe a big squeeze. "I'm naming her Chloe because that rhymes with Zoie." She made her declaration in a sing-song fashion, then grinned up at Natalie. "We've been studying rhymes at school and I like rhymes. All the time," she added, then giggled.

"I see that."

"Why are you here?" Matthew asked, since she'd made such a point to avoid him.

"To see Zoie," Carrie answered for her with a "duh" expression.

"I…" Natalie paused, then met his gaze. "I needed to talk to you about what you said to me, and when I went to your house and you weren't home I went to your mom's and she said you were here." Her face pinched nervously. "So, here I am."

"You went to my mom's?"

She nodded. "Did you mean it when you said you were falling for me?"

Matthew sent a look to his sister, who was watching the exchange curiously, as were three little pairs of eyes.

"Girls, let's go get that ice cream." A round of cheers went up at Elaine's suggestion. "I'll take your little rhymer home with me afterward." She leaned over and gave Natalie a little hug. "Good to see you again."

Before Matthew could say a word, Elaine had all three girls rushing off.

"Sorry," Natalie apologized, looking hesitant as she met his gaze. "I probably shouldn't have blurted that out."

Looking around at the semi-crowded zoo exhibit, Matthew raked his hands through his hair and nodded. "Probably not, since it no longer matters. Dr. Luiz called. I know you're leaving."

Natalie would be okay with the ground opening up and swallowing her. Surely that would be preferable to Matthew staring at her as if he *wished* she'd disappear?

"Can we go somewhere and talk?" She needed to speak to him, to explain everything swirling in her head.

Her head?

Ha. More like that wildly thumping organ beating against her ribcage.

"What's the point?" His eyes had that dark and dangerous quality to them. The one she'd first seen at the airport. Now she knew the look had been related to flying for the first time since his friends' death.

This was her fault, she reminded herself. Her fear had done this. Easily her fear could have her turning, leaving, and never risking his further rejection.

But fear couldn't win this time. She wouldn't let it.

"If we go talk," she said as calmly as she could, "I'll explain what my point is."

He looked ready to refuse, then shrugged. "Fine. Let's go."

* * *

Natalie's hands shook as she unlocked her car doors, as she climbed inside, Matthew getting in on the passenger side.

Without a word she started the car, took off down the road, not sure where she was going until she pulled into his driveway.

He hadn't said a word during the drive and didn't speak as he climbed out of the car and went to open his front door.

Natalie followed. Closing the door behind her, she went into his living room. He stood at the window, staring out.

"What did Dr. Luiz say to you?"

He didn't turn toward her, just continued to look out the window. "That you'd been offered a job out of state and had turned in your notice."

"He didn't tell me he was going to tell you."

"*You* should have told me." His tone dripped with accusation.

"I was going to, but I needed to tell Dr. Luiz first."

At that Matthew turned, met her gaze with hurt blue ones. "Seriously? You needed to tell him first?"

"For whatever it's worth, I didn't put in for another job. The university contacted me."

"It was only a matter of time before you left." He turned back to the window. "He also told me to fix whatever was between us and convince you to stay."

"Well, you're doing a bang-up job," she said sarcastically.

His gaze narrowed. "You want me to grovel?"

"No." She didn't. She wanted… "I want you to love me."

"So you can break my heart? No, thanks."

"I don't want to break your heart, Matthew. I want to claim it as my own."

"Right. You suddenly realize you can't live without me but have agreed to move to another state." He gave a sarcastic laugh. "You expect me to rip Carrie up and go with you? Is that it?"

No, she didn't expect that, didn't want that, but heard herself asking, "Would you go with me if I asked?"

His expression was gaunt. "Are you asking?"

Natalie's heart pounded in her chest. "I am."

He raked his fingers through his hair. "Moving away from Memphis would throw my life, Carrie's life, into complete chaos. You know that?"

She nodded. She knew exactly what she was

asking, what the implications of whatever answer he gave were.

Regarding her, his expression unreadable, he crossed his arms. "Tell me why I should agree to go."

Because she needed to know that he would. That he'd throw his life into utter chaos again just to be with her.

"Because of whatever this is between us, because of the way you feel about me." She took a deep breath. "Because of the way I feel about you. I love you."

There—she'd said the words out loud. No beating about the bush. She'd told him the truth. She loved him.

"I want everything you're willing to give me," she continued.

"Then my answer is yes."

She couldn't have heard him right. "Yes?"

"I'll go with you, but hell, Natalie, this isn't going to be easy on Carrie. Or me." He raked his fingers through his hair. "Plus, I'll have to figure a way out of my contract with Memphis Children's and—"

Not quite believing what he'd said, what it meant, about to burst with giddy happiness, she walked over and put her fingers over his mouth, silencing him. "You don't need to do any of those things. I shouldn't have said you did."

His eyes narrowed.

"There's no need for you to go with me because I'm not going anywhere."

He studied her. "You're not taking the job?"

She shook her head. "Why would I do that when everything I want is in Memphis?" To emphasize her point, she stood on her tiptoes and pressed a kiss to his lips. "When you and Carrie are in Memphis."

"You're sure?"

"Positive. I love you, Matthew."

"I love you, too." He pulled her to him. "Is this really happening?"

"I think so." She smiled. "I may just be the happiest woman who ever lived."

He grinned. "That happy, eh?"

"Happier."

"Good, because I want to make you happy."

"I want to be a part of your and Carrie's life, Matthew. I want to do right by her."

"Then that'll be two of us trying to do right by her, Natalie, because I'm learning as I go with this whole parenting thing."

"You're wonderful, Matthew. I watch you with her and think how lucky she is to have you, how I wish I'd had someone like you in my life."

"I'm sorry about your parents, Natalie. I wish you'd had me in your life, too. Carrie is lucky because she gets both of us to love her and make sure she always feels wanted."

"I have you now and for that, for you, I am grateful." She laid her head against her chest, listening to his heart beat, peace coming over her that, whatever life threw at them, they would handle it. Together.

"I know something that would make me very happy this very moment."

"What's that?"

"You kissing me."

Matthew was happy to oblige—then, and every day for the rest of their lives.

* * * * *

LET'S TALK

Romance

For exclusive extracts, competitions
and special offers, find us online:

📘 facebook.com/millsandboon

📷 @millsandboonuk

🐦 @millsandboon

Or get in touch on 0844 844 1351*

For all the latest titles coming soon,
visit millsandboon.co.uk/nextmonth

*Calls cost 7p per minute plus your phone company's price per
minute access charge

Want even more
ROMANCE?

Join our bookclub today!

'Mills & Boon books, the perfect way to escape for an hour or so.'

Miss W. Dyer

'Excellent service, promptly delivered and very good subscription choices.'

Miss A. Pearson

'You get fantastic special offers and the chance to get books before they hit the shops'

Mrs V. Hall

**Visit millsandbook.co.uk/Bookclub
and save on brand new books.**

MILLS & BOON